CREEZY

Félicien Marceau

CREEZY

TRANSLATED FROM THE FRENCH

BY J. A. UNDERWOOD

THE ORION PRESS   NEW YORK   1970

*This book was set on the linotype
in DeVinne. The display type is Bulmer.
It was composed, printed, and
bound at Kingsport Press, Tennessee.
Designed by Jacqueline Schuman.*

CREEZY

It's round, this plaza. No, it isn't round. Why did I say it was round? It's like all the plazas at the former gates of Paris— Porte Maillot, Porte d'Italie, Porte de Pantin—a vast open space, disproportionately large, tacked together anyhow, seeping away in all directions, losing itself in the wide avenues that run into it, ultimately shapeless, too huge for its overall plan to be discernible, its outlines blurred even further by the surging mass of traffic. You'd have to be in a helicopter. I'm not in a helicopter. I'm standing here by the curb at the edge of a pavement which is itself disproportionately large, like a beach. A beach beside a river of cars. I haven't stood still for a long time. I feel as if I haven't stood still for centuries. I was always pushed for time. Pushed in all directions. Or else I was waiting. People, things, they don't exist when you're waiting. You skirt around them, brush past them; they're not there, not really there.

I haven't got my car. I feel widowed without my car. Lost, isolated, insecure. I've left it in that garage across the way. A noise in the engine was worrying me. It's nothing much, apparently. It'll take them half an hour. This half hour lies before me like a gaping hole. Like empty space. There's nothing before me but this plaza, blurred, congested, reeling beneath the mass of cars, but empty. Only a week ago, even for this half hour, I'd have taken a taxi, I'd have gone to be with Creezy, or I'd have gone to a café to phone her. Standing in that narrow box, squeezed between the receiver and the engraved glass door, with her on the end of the line.

Creezy is no more. Do you understand that—Creezy is no more. I'm empty, vacant, uninhabited—free, yes, but in the wrong sense of the word, like a taxi which is free only when it's no longer fulfilling its function as a taxi. This woman about to walk past me—if she looks at me I could follow her. She does not look at me. I don't follow her. But I could have. I could have spared the time. I never had time until now. My time was Creezy. Every hour I managed to save—Creezy. My freedom—Creezy.

Creezy is no more. My freedom, now, is this woman walking past. Or another one. My freedom has become anything, anything at all. Shapeless. Boundless. Like this place. Reeling, pitching—where nothing either stops or exists. I see nothing before me but days without Creezy, stripped of everything that was Creezy, empty of Creezy, like huge skeletons against an ashen sky. All that is left are the . . . the things, for want of a vaguer word, among which I've been wandering for months now with no more presence than a ghost—my house, my wife (no, not even my wife any more), my children, my mail, the sessions of the Assembly, of the Finance Committee —all the things which were already crumbling beneath me and which, in order to be with Creezy, I nibbled and gnawed away at, cutting them increasingly out of my life. And which now I can only glimpse very far off, like shadows, not even that, like the shadow of a cloud which is already dispersing. Perhaps this is what despair is, this desert, this emptiness, this wearing away of everything around me, this distance between me and things, this indifference, this utter absence of any reason for going one way rather than another, for doing this thing any more than that. Once, a long time ago now, when I was in the service, my plane landed in the desert, the real one. I mean the Sahara. And I became aware that, where there should have been the well-defined runways of an airport, there was nothing but an absolutely uniform emptiness, and that the pilot was preparing to touch down precisely anywhere, there being no marks, no landing lights, not even a bush, to indicate that he should land there rather than anywhere else. I, now, am that desert. That smooth surface, that infinite emptiness with nothing sticking up or inviting attention, nothing to show the way, its very shape indeterminate, fluctuating, at the mercy of the wind, that desert is within me, a desert which is not only Creezy's absence but which is Creezy herself, that bare, arid universe she drew me into.

I am suddenly aware that I've been in this plaza before. Creezy arranged to meet me here once. She was to come and pick me up in her car. I'd parked mine over there, farther up the street. But it's just as if I'd never been here. I saw nothing of the plaza itself. I was waiting for Creezy to come in her car. I only looked at the cars. And of the cars themselves I only needed to notice one detail, the make, the color, a man driving, before they passed out of my mind and ceased to exist, and I no longer saw them.

I see them now. From one second to the next, I've begun to see them again. People, buildings, cars, all these things swim slowly and gently to the surface and float there, still rocking, before my eyes. I see the garage. I saw it before, of course, since I drove in there, but I didn't really see it, any more than I saw it that day I waited for Creezy on this very plaza. It's a large white oblong building with a longer oblong annex beside it, both parts being covered with blue writing. The attendant's uniform is blue too, but a different blue, cornflower-blue, a pastel shade. On his chest is a green and white shield, the same as the huge one which can be seen twenty feet above him, hanging, as if projected there, from a tall, curved, white boom, and joined to the garage by two strings of little flags. The whole thing sparkles, and it was this glitter which finally got through to me. The attendant has just finished wiping a windshield. He goes into his kiosk, a round kiosk, built entirely of glass, with yellow boxes stacked on shelves. Next to it stands a gas tank, painted red with a broad white rectangle. And next to that an Aston Martin, also red. Then, beyond the garage, there is a very tall building, it must have sixteen or eighteen stories, painted white but already discolored with black streaks. A man is leaning from a balcony. He is listening to a woman who is talking to him from the balcony below. She is half turned around, looking up, holding on to the balustrade with one hand. Between the balconies is an ornamental motif—a chessboard pattern, probably of tiles, white and chestnut-brown.

I'm standing near a traffic light. A taxi stops in front of me. The driver has his dog with him. They're sitting side by side. The driver strokes the dog's head, says something to it, then looks up, sees me staring at him, smiles and nods. I understand everything he is trying to tell me as clearly as if he'd spoken: the dog is his pal, he's not going to leave it at home alone all day waiting for him, it may be silly but you have to see it his way. The dog looks at me too. The taxi drives off again but it did, for a moment, exist for me. The dog, the driver, the taxi, all those things were with me.

Off to my right there is a building site with a building under construction, fenced all around, and a huge orange crane, bright orange, with its long jib, counterpoised with a block of concrete, moving slowly across the sky. I feel a kind of happiness, I don't know why, seeing this long jib slowly sweeping around. There's a cement mixer, too, or something, some machine, a motor. And there's a lot of noise. Noise which

I couldn't hear up to now, or wasn't aware of. Now I hear it. Bangs, thuds, a puffing sound, clanking, a man whistling, another calling out, I can see him, he's wearing a white helmet and yellow oilskins. It feels as if I am emerging from all this noise, as if it's a sort of grotto, or a tunnel, or a cavern, a cavern which is myself, which is this despair, which is this dreadful thing in me and I am at last emerging from it, coming out into the open air. This noise takes me out of myself, invades me, moves within me, and slowly and relentlessly crushes the dreadful thing. It feels as if a muted battle is going on inside me between this noise and my despair; I am aware of each blow, it's as if I can see my despair, as if I can see it still resisting the blows, writhing about, at last giving way, subsiding, disappearing.

A woman goes past with a little boy in tow. The little boy is clutching a red and yellow plastic machine gun. The machine gun can do nothing for him. He drags it behind him. He looks worn out. I must have had the same expression when my parents took me out with them on Sundays. The worn-out look of little boys on Sunday outings. It was always the same outing. We used to leave Morlan by the Cahors road. We stopped at a tea garden. My father would buy me a lemonade. It came in a white bottle, sealed with a marble. Now Morlan too comes back to me. Morlan comes and stands between the dreadful thing and me. I'd forgotten Morlan.

Creezy's man could never have been born in Morlan. He could only be a man in her image, the same as her, born nowhere and at no time, with no childhood, no memories, brought into the world by a computer; two robots, we were two robots, walking toward each other with a squeak of metal.

A man stops his car in front of me. He gets out. He looks at one of his wheels, the right-hand front wheel. What's the matter with his wheel? He gives his tire a kick. Then he drives off again. In the next car sit a man and a woman. She's ugly, with a pinched profile like an eel. She's talking, gesticulating. The man nods his head: yes, yes. He obviously doesn't give a damn. It doesn't matter. What matters is that all these things, the eel, the crane, the dog, the driver, the noise, the cars, little by little, all these things cover me, protect me, lull me, like a caress, like a poultice, and with this caress the dreadful thing inside me goes away, dissolves away beneath the wheels, beneath the cars, beneath the sun.

The sun is shining—I've just this minute noticed. Was it shining the day I met Creezy here, on this same plaza? I don't know. Probably I never knew. She stopped over there, twenty yards from where I'm standing now. She pulled up with a jerk, the way she always did, savagely, her haughty smile bright in the shadow of the car. I got in. She drove off just as savagely, and Creezy leaned over toward me, laughed, and shook her hair in my face.

Suddenly the dreadful thing is back inside me. I can no longer see the cars, no longer hear the rapid puffing of the motor. There is only Creezy now, Creezy with her golden profile, Creezy saying "cheese," Creezy with her wide, green eyes, Creezy my painted icon, Creezy in her long, slim, white pants, Creezy walking towards me with her model's walk, placing her heels firmly, looking straight ahead, her smile showing all her teeth, Creezy in the dead of night, her arm across my chest, her knee on my stomach, Creezy and my despair, Creezy and the dreadful thing inside me, this death, this frost, this terror, this claw, this leaden stiffening of the limbs. How is it these people don't turn around as they pass? How can they not see that, here at the curb, on the edge of this plaza reeling beneath its load of cars, a man is screaming, dragging himself along on the ground, beating the asphalt with his fists? Does nothing show on my face? Is that possible? Nothing of this panic? Nothing of this terror, this dizziness? I'm struggling, straining, I brace myself, I'm trying to breathe, I manage it at last. Once more I can hear the noise of the motor, I can hear the hiss of the tires, and with their caress the dreadful thing slowly goes away.

I am back in the world of men, back in this congested, shapeless plaza where there is nothing of Creezy, where none of the cars is like her little sports car, where none of the women has her haughty profile, or her black leather thigh boots, or her absinthe suits. I've emerged from her world, that smooth, bare, arid world of white walls, glass partitions, plastic, aluminum, steel, that plateau revolving slowly to a sound like tearing silk, that white, empty light, that universe outside which it seemed she couldn't live. Our first meeting even, at the airport. No. Careful. In what I have to say I don't know what's important and what is not. I must forget nothing, overlook nothing, even things that may appear trifling. Everything counts. If I am to recover eventually, if the dreadful thing is eventually to leave me, it will be in spite of myself, without my knowing it, it will be because I shall have chanced upon the word, the phrase, the memory, which has the power to set me free.

Before the encounter at the airport, there was the encounter at the theater which prefigured it and without which the encounter at the airport might not have been the same, even though, at the theater, we didn't speak to one another. Betty and I had gone to see the Webley play. Afterward we had arranged to meet Colette Dubois, who was in it. Betty and Colette are childhood friends. Morlan again. One a big, sensible girl with a broad face and a tender look in her blue eyes, and the other, Colette, with her boyish haircut, who used to madden us all and make fun of everybody. At the intermission we went to say hello to her. The stage manager told me they were running through an earlier scene again and that Colette was still on stage. She beckoned us to join her. I was interested to see from close up or rather from inside the set I'd been looking at from a distance. It was complicated, made entirely of steel, with revolving columns and a platform that went up and down. The producer explained to me a bit about it. Then, through a hole in the curtain, a round hole edged with leather, I had a look at the auditorium. Some of the members of the audience were standing with their backs to me, others were still in their seats. And there, in the third row, I saw a face. A face I recognized but couldn't place. Colette and Betty were talking nearby. I took Colette by the elbow.

"There, in the third row, straight in front of us, that girl in silver lamé."

Leaning on my arm, Colette looked through the hole. Then she gave one of her cooing exclamations. "Her? That's Creezy." Adding, "Creezy—*you* know. The posters. She's the only one you see nowadays."

I looked again, and it was as if everything, the auditorium, the audience, the boxes, the wreaths of lamps along the balconies, had disappeared from one second to the next. It was like a photograph in which, by means of some acid or other, everything had been toned down except for that face, just that face, surrounded by a hazy blur. I looked at her. She was looking at me. Or rather she was looking straight toward me, toward the curtain that hid me—a look that didn't see me but was totally given up to me, even more than if she had been able to see me, a look that was stripped even of that defensiveness you have when you know you're looking at someone. And the face came nearer and nearer, growing bigger and bigger, blown up as on all the posters where I had of course seen it hundreds of times—Creezy standing beside a washing machine, Creezy water skiing in an orange bikini, leaping the crest of a wave, come to the Bahamas, Creezy in an evening gown standing beside a gold cigarette lighter as tall as herself, Creezy dazzling against a background of holiday bungalows, come to the Comoro Islands, Creezy on the billboards, Creezy against the sky, Creezy twenty feet high, Creezy in banana-yellow Bermudas. Then the stage manager came forward making clapping motions with his hands and told us it was time to get back to our seats. We returned to the auditorium. The lights had already gone down. For a second, a long way off, I caught another glimpse of Creezy's profile. Afterward we left with Colette and I forgot Creezy.

Or I thought I'd forgotten her. I didn't know then that that face had stayed with me, that that haughty profile was already engraved inside my head. Occasionally the face would come back for a moment. One day, waiting at a traffic light, I looked up. The poster leapt out at me, a gigantic poster, Creezy on the crest of a wave beneath a pale sky threaded with streamers. Another time someone mentioned her at a dinner party. Again I saw the face, the theater, the wreaths of lamps. Then, a year later, exactly a year later, I had to go to Rome for a Common Market conference. The next day I left for home. There were several people with me at the airport, two deputies, the president of the Franco-Italian Section, together with an airline stewardess and a photographer. The photographer was showing off a bit, walking backwards in front of us, with a camera where his face ought to have been. We were moving through the airport lounge, a vast corridor, a vast aquarium, curved like a bow, with huge windows, walls of mica forming glittering caves, the thunder of jet engines, breathless voices, caressing voices, inhuman voices, announcing, as if it were the most precious secret, that the flight for Caracas was now leaving from gate number twelve and that Mr. Smith, flight seven two two, was requested . . . but for what? For what delights? The breathless voices promised delights. For whose embrace? The breathless voices promised embraces or farewells of excruciating sweetness.

Then it happened: I saw Creezy, Creezy walking toward me with her model's walk, walking toward me from the far end of the vast lounge, through the breathless, inhuman voices, through the thunder of the jets, she too flanked by people, two men, a woman, an airline stewardess, she too with a photographer walking backwards in a crouched position. It

9

was strange, comical, disturbing, those two groups advancing toward each other, in step, as in a mirror; it was a trick with mirrors, as in a maze, identical except for details, our charcoal-gray suits, Creezy in her white thigh boots and leopard-skin coat, flowers too, she was carrying a spray of flowers, roses, bound with silver paper. At one point, still retreating backwards, our two photographers crossed, and for several seconds they looked as if they were photographing each other. I smiled at Creezy. She didn't smile. Or rather she didn't alter the smile she'd had all along, a set smile, her poster smile, but I saw a ripple pass across her face, as if she was smiling far off behind her smile. One of the photographers beckoned us to move closer. He wanted to take us both together. The president of the Franco-Italian Section was annoyed. "No, no," he said. "It wouldn't do, what an idea!" He must have thought it would compromise the dignity of a French deputy. There was a fuss. A third airline stewardess came up. It seemed we were late, they were waiting for us, all the other passengers had already boarded the plane. I shook a few hands at random. As Creezy went through the gate, she thrust her flowers into the arms of the ticket inspector. He looked rather astonished but said thank you. We walked side by side toward the plane, the stewardess a couple of steps in front of us, turning around every now and then as if to make sure we were being good. We were being good. Creezy beside me, Creezy in her leopard-skin coat, Creezy was walking into my life, I knew it already, walking into my life with her model's walk, slipping the foot forward slightly, moving rather like a ship.

In the plane, it was quite natural for us to sit together. We were given the two front seats on the right. There was no one in front of us. We were alone, alone in that case of humming steel, alone with the remarks we exchanged, each of which already meant something else, and we knew it, the words feeling their way between us, seeking each other out, and we

and very large. I mean, for each large window—or more exactly, wall of glass—there were two windows of ordinary size. In front of the building, a lawn, three circular flowerbeds, a blue tiled basin with a meager fountain playing in it, and a path made of irregularly laid paving stones. I believe architects call it *opus incertum*. The whole thing was so banal it was actually disturbing. Venturing along the *opus incertum* path, I felt I was walking through a prospectus, on my way to see a speculator. The lawn didn't look real. It was an acid green color, suggestive not so much of nature as of some chemical process. In the plane I'd told Creezy the story about the Detroit woman who got a divorce because once while she was out her husband had had a plastic lawn put down in the garden; he hadn't told her about it and had let her go on watering it for six months. Creezy didn't laugh. I needed to find out what made her laugh. I felt strongly that there was something in her I must break down, unravel, something hard, knotted. Making her laugh would be one way.

I entered the lobby. The concierge's lodge was a fortress, a redoubt, built entirely of glass, S-shaped, with plants everywhere, all along the curved wall and right up to the ceiling, broad, shiny, dark green leaves which looked as if they were made of plastic. The concierge bobbed up from behind this manufactured foliage and answered my query through a pane of glass riddled with holes. The only human note in the whole scene was the jumper the concierge was knitting, a blue woollen cardigan, quite astonishing. You'd sooner have expected to find a radar screen in that glass cell, or a laser gun or a Geiger counter. No, just a jumper. Nothing remarkable about the elevator, just a metal box, except that syrupy music was coming out of a loudspeaker.

At Creezy's apartment on the twelfth floor a tall woman opened the door. She was against the light and in any case I hardly gave her a glance because Creezy was already coming toward me from the big room off the hall. She seemed to be emerging from the huge window wall behind her, which framed her with a halo of light. She held out a hand to me.

"How kind of you," she said.

Kind? The polite formula took me by surprise. "I said I'd come."

She wasn't listening. "This is my Spanish woman," she said.

I turned to the woman who had let me in. She had a large bony face with a strong nose, a stubborn mouth, and big bulging eyes which were staring at me. She was wearing a long severe housecoat with a military collar, made of some soft blue material that looked like oilcloth. It didn't suit her at all. Her bones seemed to shift under her skin and her face moved into what must have been a smile. For no reason at all I said, "Well done." What was well done?

"She's called Snow," said Creezy, adding, "I can't stand foreign names so I've translated it."

I said, "How do you do, Snow."

Snow had done her smile. She wasn't smiling again. We stood there for a moment, waiting for something. What, we didn't know. Creezy watching me. Snow impassive. I seemed to be hovering. I get like that sometimes. When my attention wanders, or when I have to make an effort to remember what I'm thinking about. It was as if all three of us were absent, somewhere else. As if, in the no-man's land of that hall, we were wondering which way everything was going to swing.

Finally Creezy went into the big room. I followed her. That day she was wearing orange pants, a lime-green turtle-neck sweater, and a gold belt consisting of several chains. I told her the apartment was like the airport. It was like the airport. As bare, as empty, and even in a way as vast. The huge window wall covered the whole of one end. There was a door open in the middle of it. Outside there was a balcony. The main room or living area (I can't stand the phrase but I

14

don't have another one) comprised two stories, which explained the curious distribution of windows already mentioned, the smaller windows corresponding to the rooms which are only half the height, the kitchen and bathroom. Opposite the window wall a steel staircase led up to a gallery which constituted another room, above the hall. In the main room there was a table, fixed to the wall by the narrow end in such a way that it could be folded up. It was up then and on the reverse side was pasted an enormous photograph of Creezy, a brutal shot, cut off above the eyes and at the chin, gray and black, grainy, like some kind of ogress. In addition there was a television, a record player, a long narrow divan, and a lamp, or I should say a piece of lighting equipment, consisting of a metal frame and a number of white tubes pointing in different directions. And in one corner lay a pile of records, telephone books, record jackets, and suitcases. The carpet was slate-gray. The walls lemon-yellow. Stuck up on the right-hand wall was the washing-machine poster; on the left-hand wall the Bahamas poster, Creezy water skiing, leaping through the foam; on the end wall, Creezy in banana-yellow Bermudas against a background of holiday bungalows, come to the Comoro Islands.

Creezy was standing in front of the Bahamas poster. It was as if her shadow had been projected onto the wall behind her, disproportionately large, the way a spotlight would throw it—no, not her shadow, that's not right, not strong enough, it was as if she herself had been projected there, had been torn from herself, stolen from herself, transformed into that giant rushing toward us out of a sky threaded with streamers. Ice cubes clinked in my glass. Suddenly it seemed to me that Creezy, with that giant showing all around her, didn't exist any more, or that she was everywhere, that I was in a city where the buildings were so many Creezys, in a room where the walls were so many Creezys, all advancing toward me, closing in on me, Creezy in the foam of the waves, Creezy in the sky threaded with streamers. The ice cubes clinked again.

The dream faded. The posters retreated. Only Creezy herself was left. I thought: Do I still want her? Nothing was left of the thrill I had felt at the airport, had felt even in the car coming there, and which, oddly, had dissolved as I walked along the *opus incertum* path. I felt only the most coarse of all emotions—male pride.

I moved toward Creezy. I took her by the elbows. She broke away. I seized her again. She placed a hand on my chest. The hand holding her glass. It wasn't a caress, it was to push me away. I took her glass. I looked for some place to put it down: there was nothing. I finally put it on the floor. Mine as well. Creezy hadn't moved. She was looking at me. She bit her lip. I leaned toward her. My cheek touched hers.

"There's Snow," she said.

Snow? "But she's in the kitchen."

"She might come in."

"Send her out shopping."

I very distinctly saw a rude answer taking shape in Creezy's green eyes. It took shape. It didn't come out. I stepped back and said in a formal tone of voice, "I wonder if I might ask a favor of you. Could you lend me Snow for an hour?"

Her green eyes showed a flicker of interest. "What do you want her for?"

Lying on top of the pile of records was a telephone book listed according to streets. I looked under Rue de Charonne. I found a Mr. Coutelet. Coutelet, F. Just that.

"I wonder if I could have an envelope, too. And a sheet of paper."

The flicker of interest was still there. Creezy handed me the envelope and the sheet of paper.

"I want her to take a letter to this Mr. . . . ." I'd already forgotten the name. I picked up the phone book again. "To this Mr. Coutelet."

"But . . . do you know him?"

"No. Not at all."

"Well, what are you going to write to him?"

"Nothing. I'm sending him the sheet of paper, that's all. My only interest in him is the fact that his address is Rue de Charonne. On the other side of Paris."

"Oh, no!"

I'd hoped to make Creezy laugh. She didn't laugh. But she was more lively. That was something.

"It's silly to send a blank sheet of paper. You ought to write . . . wait a minute . . . write, 'All is discovered, run for it.' "

"Suppose the man has really . . . No, no, I wouldn't want to have it on my conscience. I'm going to write . . ."

All the ice, the cold, the frostiness between us had disappeared. Creezy pulled me across the room by the hand and lowered the table so that I could write on it.

"I'm going to say, 'You are urgently requested to telephone . . .' " It was inadequate, I knew. "Imagine his face . . . Wait . . . I'll sign it, 'Joshua.' "

I tried to find the idea of Joshua irresistibly funny. It wasn't. All Creezy's animation had subsided, from one second to the next.

"Snow can hardly speak a word of French. She'll never find it."

"I'll call for a taxi. The taxi can take her and bring her back." Creezy looked at me. Again that absence was between us. "You surely can't refuse me this favor?"

Creezy called Snow. She explained it to her. In Spanish. Rapid, jerky Spanish. For some reason her Spanish made me uneasy. It was like another Creezy, a dimension of Creezy, a life of Creezy, about which I knew nothing. I went out on the balcony. I saw the taxi approaching down the empty street. The driver was hesitant, turning the wheel this way and that, shaking his head as if he couldn't believe his eyes at having to venture so far into the unknown. He looked, in that desert, like a cockroach wandering across the tiled floor of a kitchen. I went down in the elevator with Snow. She was wearing a gray velours overcoat and her face was tense and serious.

I gave the driver his instructions. Snow was already sitting in the taxi, her handbag on her knees and her hands on top of it. I was suddenly worried she might take it into her head to hand the letter to Mr. Coutelet in person. I tried to explain to her. I was wasting my breath. She said, "Yes, yes," but it was obvious she didn't understand a word. I tried to retrieve my letter from her handbag but she wouldn't let me, retreating to the far end of the seat. I finally got hold of it and gave it to the driver. I told him simply to hand it to the concierge.

"Right you are," said the driver.

Snow said, "*Vamos.*"

But then the driver caught up with me. "Here, in that case there's no need for the lady to come along."

"Yes, yes, she must."

The driver began to turn nasty. He was a youngish man, round-faced, wearing a leather jacket. "Don't you trust me?"

Life is sometimes tricky. "I trust you but the lady has to go to Rue de Charonne."

"If you don't trust me you'd better say so now."

Then he gave a start. Snow had just slapped him on the shoulder. She said, "*Vamos.*"

"All right," said the driver. "Fine, I'll say no more about it." He was like Creezy. For a moment he'd been interested in my problem. He wasn't interested any more. The taxi drove off. Snow gave me a final wave out the window.

From her aquarium the concierge watched me pass. I got back to the apartment. I ran to Creezy. No, there was still something wrong, but what was it? I took her in my arms. She was quite stiff. I kissed her neck. Her neck was stiff, her spine hard. I spoke. She said no. No. No. She shook her head. Placing both hands flat on my chest she pushed me away.

18

"Snow has gone now."

"It's not just Snow," she said.

"Why did you let her go, then?"

"What do you mean?" she said. "It was you who wanted it."

This piece of hypocrisy made me very annoyed. I picked up my glass. Creezy picked up hers. They hung like a thousand miles between us, those two glasses.

"May I kiss you, at least?"

She made a gesture of irritation and then said, "I can see no reason why I shouldn't kiss you."

But the kiss led nowhere. A nothing kiss. I felt only emptiness. My one desire was to go away. I tried to pull myself together. How many men, seeing her posters, had dreamed of Creezy? I had Creezy before me. But in what way, for me, was she any more real than her posters? At least in the posters there was movement, a luster, a smile. There was none of that in the woman who stood beside me, holding her glass, cheerless, wrapped up in herself, buried in I knew not what. I thought of Snow. Snow, the taxi, the driver, rushing across Paris to deliver a message that meant nothing. To deliver a little bit of nothingness. The same nothingness that had slipped between Creezy and me in that bleak and brand-new room.

I felt a surge of anger, anger I gladly welcomed, anger that made me sure of myself again. I stood up. I leaned over Creezy. I seized her by the wrists. She looked me up and down. Her expression was stubborn, obdurate. No. I must use all the words: her expression was sullen, she looked bored stiff.

I said, "Are you bored?"

She said, "No."

I said "Would you like me to go?"

"No," she said.

A trace of impulse, that time. I pulled her by the wrists. She struggled. She was stronger than I'd expected. I finally got her to her feet. I dragged her toward the staircase. Suddenly she broke free. She climbed the staircase with a resolute step. We went into her room. No, we didn't go in and it wasn't a room. There was no door. The gallery overlooked the living area with only a balustrade separating them. Between the staircase at one end and a door leading to the bathroom at the other, there was simply a space, without definition and with no particular beginning and no particular end. The furniture looked as if it had been left there temporarily: the bed, a bedside table, the telephone, a lamp with an ivory-colored shade, a dressing table trimmed with white satin, a featureless, eyeless, pale green head on which a wig rested, and, right at the back, a filing cabinet, a regular office filing cabinet, dark green. For intimacy the place rated nil.

Scattered on the bed were twenty-five or thirty cushions, little square cushions, all identical, with pink and turquoise stripes. Creezy picked them up and started throwing them anywhere. I gathered them up. I made a pile of them. They formed a sort of wall—a suggestion, a symbol of a wall. Creezy took off her sweater. Her gaze swept over me without pausing, like a lighthouse beam. I took off my jacket. I went over to her to undo the zip fastener of her orange pants. She didn't look up. She watched my hand on the zip fastener. She in her long slim white pants and I in my short pants—we looked as if we were getting ready for a judo match, not for love. One sentence might have saved us. It didn't come. Or a smile. Neither of us smiled. We made love. Making love is usually a pretty good way of getting to know one another. We didn't get to know one another.

| *three*

That was a Friday. On the Sunday I went there again. I told Betty I had to go on an official trip. I arrived at Creezy's apartment. Snow wasn't there. On Sundays she used to go to the Spanish church and then spend the day with friends. I took Creezy out to lunch in the country. She wanted to take her car. It irritated her to be driven by someone else; she couldn't bear it. She herself drove like a maniac, in leaps and bounds, like a jaguar. Whenever she had a hundred yards of clear road she took off as if it were a parkway. Her car could do it. It was an M. 19. That's a lively car. Black, with a long hood. At traffic lights Creezy braked in the space of a yard, and every time it made her laugh, or at least her lips would pucker. And as we started off again, engine snarling, she'd lean over toward me, shaking her hair in my face, and her cheek would linger against mine for a moment.

On the way back we passed a path that led away between the trees. I suggested we stop.

"You're not going to tell me you like the country?"

There was a note of fathomless scorn in her voice. I insisted I loved the country. I launched into a lecture on trees: there's something about trees, a peace of mind, of heart; an oak tree is like a cathedral. Reluctantly Creezy got out of her car. After ten yards things were already improving. In the end she loved the country too. But it was obvious she knew nothing about it. When I plucked one of those grasses that stick to your clothes and put it on her back, she went mad. She hadn't known there was such a thing. She stuck them all over me, on my legs, my chest, even a crown of them on my head. I looked like a walking bush. She threw herself into my arms. We kissed amid the grasses sticking to our clothes. I taught her the difference between the nettles that sting and the ones that don't sting. I showed her those little leaves that, when you throw them up in the air, come down spinning. She was delighted by everything. "Clever gadgets," she called them. She was fairly sensibly dressed that day: a suit with broad pink and brown chevrons and a large, crude-looking brooch. We found a stream. I started skipping stones. I hoped she would be impressed. She wasn't at all impressed. But my enjoyment seemed to amuse her.

"You're fifteen again," she said.

On the Friday, in spite of everything, we had made love. Then it hadn't helped us. Now it did. Creezy was no longer either obdurate or sullen. She was laughing and talking non-stop as she climbed her steel staircase. And laughing as she threw me the cushions from her bed. I built my little wall. We were like a couple of bricklayers tossing bricks to one another. Then, when we were almost undressed, we kissed, very tenderly. She pulled off my pants. I pulled off hers. We made love very peacefully, almost in slow motion, as if we knew it was our right. The huge window wall of the living area was a blaze of sunshine. It was as if there was no window there, only a sheet of pure light, as if we were on the threshold of a world of emptiness, on the very edge of a cliff that plunged down we knew not where, into an abyss perhaps.

I had a bath. Creezy added some purple stuff to the water that made it lather. Creezy laughed. She emptied the whole bottle. The foam rose higher and higher, over my head, I was buried in it as in a cave. Underneath, the water was blue, a rich blue, as in the Bahamas poster. Above, far off, Creezy was laughing, naked, scooping up the foam and piling it on my head, Creezy was walking away with her model's walk, she came back, I emerged from my foam, still covered in it, Creezy handed me a bathrobe, one of her bathrobes, lettuce-green, but it fit me. Creezy could have been taken for frail. She was not. She had shoulders like a boy, and on the Friday, wrestling with her, I had discovered she had the strength of a tiger.

I joined her in the living area. She had slipped on a bathrobe too, an olive-green one, very short. She was sitting on the floor, on the slate-gray carpet. She was looking at television. I looked at her, lying on the floor with my head resting on her thigh, gazing up at her. Her eyes were very wide apart, her nose straight, small but straight, neatly shaped, her chin wilful, slightly thrust forward. A hard profile. The profile of an Egyptian queen. Head held high. There's a bird that has that same way of holding its neck erect, standing very upright, a crested bird—or like those Italian or Greek women who carry baskets on their heads. A neck like a column, with a column's strength.

I started to sort out the records. That untidy pile had begun to annoy me—records, books, papers, telephone books, and dozens of pink parking tickets. She brought her records to me and I knelt on the slate-gray carpet and sorted them into various types. At one point, as she stood there handing me the records and I knelt before her, our eyes met. And an angel passed. We were one. At least, as one as it is possible to be. One in that emptiness. In that great, square, empty space between the window wall on one side and the three posters on the others. The sun and three pale skies. The sun and the three giant Creezys rushing toward me. She knelt down too, facing me at first, her bare knees showing beneath the olive-green bathrobe, then closer, gliding down beside me. A look of anxiety had come into her eyes. She seemed to be wondering what I was doing there, in her life, surrounded by her records, what part I was going to play and whether it was important. Amazement too. Did such things exist, then? Such a bond? Such a melting together? Time standing still like that in the middle of a Sunday afternoon, just because of us? What men had she met before? I never even dreamt of asking her. In Creezy's universe everything was immediate, born on the instant and gone on the instant. We had been born, she and I, she for me and, even more, I for her, in the airport, among the breathless voices and the thunder of the jets. Before that— nothing, a belt of darkness, not even that, darkness still suggests something, a limbo, a vagueness, a blur, hardly different from nothingness. Tomorrow—the idea did not even occur to us. The present lay around us, motionless, frozen, like a layer of frost. I even had to make an effort to remember the episode at the theater. One day Creezy had been there, that's all, born out of her posters, fresh from the Bahamas, from the other end of the airport lounge, already possessing her age, her Egyptian profile, her model's walk, and her erect neck like that crested bird.

She inclined her head. Her shoulder was touching mine. Her mouth clung to my mouth, her mouth was inside my mouth, and slowly, gently, we sank down on the slate-gray carpet. I entered her, was in her, her head thrashed from side to side, then for a moment she held it still, in profile against the gray carpet, as if she was listening, as if her body was listening to mine, then her mouth was in my mouth again, our bathrobes lay around us like huge wings spread out, huge dead wings, lettuce-green and olive-green, and I lifted her and her body arched against mine and I was in her as she heaved, her body like a sea swell beneath me, her heels beating the carpet, I was in her with all her muscles around me, holding me, squeezing, like an avid mouth drawing me down into the depths, and her hands, her fingers clutched at my hips and they were drawing me down too, they drew me down to the depths and beyond, they clung to my hips, I was saving a drowning girl, my Ophelia, my Creezy, I bit her neck, I could feel a little pulse there, beating fast, she tensed, reared up, her body like a strung bow, her muscles hard, her mouth in my mouth, her belly my belly, she moaned, she grunted, a short gasping grunt, her body opened, opened wider, I inside and she said, "Come, come," and I was coming, I was running, a furious gallop, a tidal wave, and I came, I yelled out, lightning shot through me, I pounced on her mouth, and in our bodies peace came like a stupor, like a sigh, us, you, me in you, my Creezy, there on the slate-gray carpet. Slowly, like two pieces of flotsam washed up by a calm sea, we rose to the surface. We emerged in the middle of that great, square, empty space between the window and the yellow walls.

Afterward we went into the kitchen. It was a beautiful kitchen, all mechanized, with ten different appliances and red Formica and white tiles with a picture on every fourth one depicting a vegetable or a ship. There wasn't much in the refrigerator—eggs, two avocado pears, some champagne. We ate on the Formica table.

I said, "This reminds me of our plane."

"What plane?" said Creezy.

We decided to go to the movies, I looked for a paper, I found one but it was a week old, we decided against the movies, or rather the idea of going to the movies eventually just faded away. Creezy put on a record and then turned it off. We wandered around vacantly. Our gestures became meaningless. We went to bed. No, even going to bed wasn't decided just like that. At one point Creezy went up to her

four   ✨

Careful. I've got to be careful. Overlook nothing. Nor go too fast, either. If there is a key, it's here somewhere. That day, that Sunday, a flash of light passed between Creezy and me. That flash must illuminate something. I'm not talking about love. I'm not even talking about spending that night together. I mean those records, that moment when our eyes met, that moment of recognition, that moment when we were one. It's not difficult in love. In that embrace, that struggle, that race, that game of hopscotch, that frozen instant of eternity, it's not difficult to be one—or to have the illusion of being so. The difficult thing is to be one while you're sorting out records. At that moment, between the window wall and the three posters, there hung a question. And on the threshold of that question we paused, and then gave the most simple, most obvious answer: we made love. Perhaps it was not enough. We let our bodies guide us. Do they always guide us well? Don't they sometimes come between us and the truth as it dances before us, passes, and disappears as quickly as it came? Bodies are clumsy things and the truth is a dancer, the truth only stands on one leg. Or was there no other answer? Or was there not really a question? It's possible. Maybe there was nothing but our two yearning bodies. Maybe there was nothing but the pomp and ceremony with which we enshrine and decorate desire, that state in which, flung up to the pinnacle of our being, we find it so easy, so natural, to talk of life and death and always and never, only to discover afterward that we are amazed at having spoken, amazed at having said such things, and sink back into our well-worn grooves. No, I am certain that in that moment with Creezy I came very close to something, I stood on the threshold of another world, on the threshold of a land I only glimpsed through the mist. But what was it I came close to? I don't know. Perhaps I'll never know. We are all actors in a play of which we never know the script and never understand it, in which our experience is of no use to us and in which happiness and unhappiness are nothing but the twin dark faces of that which eternally escapes us: the other. What I am doing is reciting that script, reciting all the gestures, directions, speeches. Others must sift and decipher it. In my hotel room . . . No, there's no point in talking about my hotel room. If there is a secret, it isn't there.

At eleven o'clock I called Creezy. I said, "I'm coming."

She replied, "Please do."

Again, the polite formula astonished me. Moreover, Creezy had delivered it in the most even tone of voice and definitely without a hint of irony. Just like the time a few days before when I had arrived at her place and she had said, "How kind of you." I'd noticed already in the plane how sometimes she would come out with a phrase that sounded completely automatic, like one of those dolls—you pull a string and they say, "Daddy. Mummy. Pretty gee-gee." Creezy was the same. Sometimes. Not often. As if she were thinking of something else, or couldn't be bothered to choose her words but took the first phrase that came into her head.

I arrived at the apartment. Snow let me in, then went back to her vacuum cleaner. Creezy was wearing geranium-colored pants and an electric-blue Chinese jacket with a little stand-up collar. She said something to me. It was drowned out by the hum of the vacuum cleaner. She walked in her determined way over to the socket, withdrew the plug, told me, "I have to go out," and put the plug back in.

I made an attempt to reply, but with that noise going on it was impossible. So I pulled the plug out too. Snow stood the handle of the vacuum cleaner upright, placed her hand on it, and waited, without a flicker of expression on her face, just like a sentry standing at ease.

"You're going out?"

"I have to."

"What about me? Why did you tell me to come?"

"Oh, you . . ." she said. "You make things so complicated. I won't be long. I've got to go pose. You can come and get me at three o'clock."

"What about our lunch?"

"We'll have lunch afterward."

"And where do I have to pick you up?"

"Place de la Concorde."

"Where in the Place de la Concorde? It's enormous." Her smile became particularly haughty then. We weren't very one that morning, certainly. All right, I thought, I'd find her. But I added just in case, "If we don't find each other, meet me back here."

I replaced the plug. Creezy darted around in the living room for a moment longer and then left. She hadn't kissed me. It's true I hadn't made any attempt at it. I'd already learned that with Creezy the present was the present. Nothing over-lapped. The present, at that moment, was not me, it was the modeling session. A kiss would have meant a memory—or a promise. They were words which meant absolutely nothing to Creezy. I went out on the balcony and watched her get into her car. A man was walking his dog in the street. When the man saw Creezy he stopped. The dog pulled on the lead. The man followed but kept his head turned toward Creezy. The car leapt into motion like a wild beast picking up a scent.

I went back inside. Snow had stopped the vacuum cleaner. It's a well-known fact that when a vacuum cleaner is no longer disturbing anyone it's lost its usefulness. She said something to me in Spanish. I didn't understand. I said, *"Si, si."* The records were still lying on the carpet exactly as we had left them. Creezy must have told Snow not to touch them. I sorted a few more of them. Then I turned on the record player. It was African music, full of dry sounds, bits of wood being banged together. I lay down on the carpet.

When I woke up all was quiet. The record player had stopped. I went into the kitchen: Snow had gone out. Once again, in that great empty cube, I had the impression of being nowhere. There were some letters lying around. It occurred to me for a moment that if I read them I might perhaps discover the thing about Creezy that was still shut off from me, secret, might find the one detail that would help me to come closer to her. I didn't do it. Once, a long time ago, I came across a letter that was not addressed to me and I read in it a passage about myself that was so unpleasant, and so true, that I swore never to do such a thing again.

I got in my car and drove to the Place de la Concorde. I needn't have worried. The first thing I saw was a crowd of people, a small crowd, in front of the Admiralty. Creezy was there. She was brandishing a golf club. There were two photographers, a bald man, a big woman with the build of a sergeant, who looked as if she knew what she was doing there, and another, more insipid woman who was holding a board with some papers clipped to it.

I pulled up. Creezy threw me a brief smile, or rather it was as it had been at the airport: she was already smiling for the photographers and, keeping that smile, she briefly crinkled her eyes and nose to let me know she'd seen me. Then she handed her golf club to the big woman, raised one forefinger in my direction, and placed the other forefinger across it, about halfway up. What did that mean? That she would be another half hour? At any rate, her gesture earned me the attention of the crowd of onlookers, who turned around toward me or rather simply turned their heads, had a good look, sized me up, and then turned back to Creezy.

An employee came up. He told me I couldn't wait there. I told him I was with Mademoiselle. He went away. I got out of my car. The sun was shining thinly through the clouds, giving a pearly light. Around me, the onlookers were passing comments.

A fat woman was saying, "Well, how's that for the fashion of the future!"

The man who was with her gave her a look and then indicated me, as if to convey to her that remarks of that sort, in my hearing, were perhaps not in the best of taste.

But the fat woman was not to be put off. "Can you see me wearing that?" she asked him.

The man replied, "Well, it's not meant for your kind of figure, is it?"

Creezy's sign couldn't have meant half an hour because she had finished. She left the photographers, the bald man, and the sergeant-woman without a word or even a handshake, exactly the way she had left me the night before to sink into sleep. One minute she was there, the next minute she wasn't, that was all. She came over to me. All the heads turned again. The question of which car came up. She had hers, I had mine.

"I'll follow behind you," she said.

And, of course, she'd hardly started off before she was fifty yards ahead of me. At the first traffic light I managed to pull in beside her. She laughed, shook out her hair, reached out her hand to me through the window.

I shouted, "Where are we going?"

She shouted back, "Wherever you like." And she was off again.

A little farther on I saw her parking her car, only slightly damaging another one; then she ran over to me and got in my car, saying she'd rather come with me and pick up her car later.

We had lunch in a snack bar where the waiters wore flowered jackets. Forget-me-nots. Creezy said she would have preferred hydrangeas because in the first place there'd be less of them. And she said, "I'm happy today, aren't you?"

"Yes, I am happy."

"I want to give you a present. What would you like? Something useful, something silly, or going to see the trees?"

"I'd like the trees best."

We went to the Parc de Saint-Cloud. We walked a little way down one of the wide avenues. Creezy clung to my arm. An old gentleman was pointing out a mushroom to a little boy, explaining to him that it wasn't the right kind. Another man went past and Creezy said he was a voyeur; she said she had an eye for that kind of thing.

We went back to the apartment. Snow was battling with a man who was trying, without any success, to convey to her that if the gas bill was not paid the supply would be cut off. I reached for my wallet. Creezy hit me on the arm. She paid the man, laughed, shook out her hair, and added a quite inordinately large tip. The man was smitten. He was ready to tell her his life story. He had a nervous twitch in the eyelids which made him look a bit dazzled anyway. She bundled him out the door very briskly, and from one second to the next all was calm again.

I sat down on the narrow divan. Creezy glided into my arms. The sun was directly opposite us in the hugh window wall. Then the sun went in. Creezy shivered, jumped up,

33

decided we would have dinner in the apartment, called Snow, spoke to her in Spanish, called a grocer, said "Please do" to him just as she had to me, without a shadow of expression.

After that she went into the bathroom. She called me. I gave her a shower. I kissed the water on her breasts, on her hips. Then she showered me. We lay down on the bed. Our bodies were as innocent as in the first days of the world.

I was already inside her when I said, "What about Snow?"

Her expression was unbelievably serious as she replied, "I spoke to her this morning. She has agreed."

Agreed? Snow?

After dinner she again became restless. She wanted to go get her car. I pointed out that . . . No, she must have her car. "My car is my home. It was you who said that."

Did I say that?

"You said it was when I was in my car that I looked most at home."

All right, I said it. I suggested we go in my car to get hers. No, Creezy wouldn't have it: that would mean we'd have to come back separately.

I called for a taxi. In the taxi Creezy snuggled up to me and I held her hand. But she talked to the driver, asking him if he liked his job, what he did during slack periods, and whether the traffic jams didn't give him nervous breakdowns. The driver was delighted. He told us he was in business for himself, that he lived in the suburbs, and that he bred rabbits. They're very affectionate, apparently. His could recognize him. According to him the rabbit is a very much misunderstood animal. As for the slack periods, he had no complaints. He read. Historical works, by preference. He'd done Louis XIII and he was now on Louis XIV. But he hadn't yet had time to form an opinion of the man. Frankly, it was too early to say.

34

He turned around toward me. "How about you, sir, just between ourselves—what do you think of him as a king?"

Creezy was in heaven. At each detail she nudged me with her knee or her hand tightened on mine. For her the present was that driver. If I'd shouted my head off I couldn't have got through that wall of rabbits and nervous breakdowns.

We arrived at where the car was. The driver got out with us. He wanted us to know that fares like ourselves were very rare, that the majority of fares didn't give a damn about the driver's health or his personal status or his problems. The Seine flowed past, sluggish in the moonlight. A metro train clattered across the bridge. The driver wanted to buy us a drink. I declined. He insisted. Creezy wanted to.

We went into a corner bar at the bottom of a street of steps. The bar was empty. Between the two glass doors stood a game, a motor circuit, with a little car twisting its way like a rat through a sleeping city. Creezy pounced on it immediately. She wrenched the little steering wheel this way and that with the force of a stevedore. Each time she did something good or made a mistake a bell rang or yellow, green, or purple lights flashed on and click, click, click, somewhere the counting mechanism started up and numbers appeared. It was like a nagging conscience, crabby and watchful. There have been any number of those lights, flashes and signals in my life. There were plenty in my life with Creezy.

The driver came up, glass in hand. He watched like a professional. He said it was tricky. Then he left. Creezy barely noticed. She was playing with feverish concentration. She didn't even take her eyes off the machine as she reached out a hand to me and said, "Another franc, please." Standing impassively behind his hard-boiled egg stand, the barman handed me more change. It was her thirty-second game. Flashing lights, bells, click, click, click, numbers appearing.

Suddenly Creezy had had enough. We went back to the

car. Creezy drove very fast. I said, "We're going the wrong way." She laughed and shook out her hair. At one point her cheek was against mine and we were heading straight for a lighted post. I felt only indifference. At the last moment Creezy swerved. I said, "Turn left." She turned right. Still at breakneck speed. We were in a long, sad, empty street, I had no idea where; I didn't recognize anything. Creezy stepped on the brake. In her usual brutal way. I went hurtling toward the windshield. She caught me. Her mouth clung to my mouth. Her whole body clung to mine.

She said, "You'll save me, won't you?"

What from? I knew I must save her but what from? I asked, "What from?"

She said, "You never understand anything." Adding, "That's not it. That's not it at all."

But what was it, then? Did she know herself? It was night, the dead of night, in an empty street that looked dead too. Were we ever anywhere else but in the night? Or in a pale light that was equally obscure? Creezy turned to reverse the car. The headlights swept across a row of houses in front of us and then lit up a billboard and, on the billboard, there was Creezy, in an orange bikini, on water skis, skimming the crest of the waves, in the Bahamas. She hurtled toward us out of a sky threaded with streamers. My heart skipped a beat. Creezy seemed unaffected. For a moment longer Creezy was before us, above us, enormous, dashing toward us as if to catch us up, hold us back. Then the car completed the turn and Creezy fell back into the night. Another street, a plaza, a bridge, the sluggish, gleaming Seine, and bang—we were on the parkway. The tunnel hummed around us. I love that—the bumps and jolts, the scream of the tires, and those bends twisting in all directions like a fireworks display. I was falling asleep. I mean: in my life. Creezy was shaking me like a cocktail. Her profile, lit by the dashboard lights and the beams of the streetlights, thrust forward hard and golden, as if it had been carved by the snarling of the engine. We left the parkway. Under the tall street lights the landscape stretched flat and gleaming, jellified in that empty glare. Trees slid past on both sides of the road. Somewhere, someone was pulling them, felling them, mowing them down.

Creezy no longer spoke. She was leaning forward, caught up in her private tunnel of noise and speed and the humming of tires. We passed through a village. The headlights picked out a white wall. It loomed up in front of us like a startled face. Then up a narrow winding lane that climbed between old, rough-hewn walls. The headlights leapt from side to side in bright bursts as if a photographer were running along in front of us madly popping bulbs. We came to a big intersection with five or six different levels. At the highest point Creezy stopped the car. We got out. Beneath us was a series of long viaducts and long curved ramps sweeping in all directions, with pillars, arches, stretches of road surface, some black, others gleaming white, and over all the white and pale gray lunar glare of the tall street lights. Beyond, all around, lay darkness. It was like being in a diving bell, but a vast one, a vast desert of concrete and steel where the air seemed somehow rarefied, a world forsaken, sealed off and frozen. We set off again. Creezy took all the curving ramps, one after another. Around and around the intersection we went, around that maze in the sky; and as we passed under the arches, the neon lights cast a greenish glare.

We took a road off to the right. A big development loomed up out of the night, cliff-like, blocks of apartments with a few windows still lit up and down below the pallid, empty glare of the street lights. We felt the car rise beneath us. A ramp led us up to a fairly large, open place surrounded by arcades, tucked away among the tall buildings. There was a bar there. At that time of night it was only half open: the main part was in shadow but there was still a yellow light burning above the bar. We went in. Three youths and the barmaid watched us from the counter. They were all leaning together, forming a sort of pyramid under the yellow light. Creezy walked with her determined step over to a game, a crane, with a few knickknacks lying on a bed of dried beans. Creezy began to operate it savagely. Where she was standing, at the edge of the zone of shadow, her face was lit only by the little window of the machine. She became impatient and gave the machine a shake. One of the youths said, "Hey, it's not a tank." The others gave a low chuckle. I could see a fight coming. I itched for one. I'd caught Creezy's madness. But at a glare from Creezy's green eyes the three youths had already turned back to the bar and were buried in their drinks. Only their backs could be seen, and the ash-blond barmaid giving me a friendly smile.

We left. There was a toy store in the arcade with all its lights on. In the window was a child's outfit, a Zorro outfit, complete with lasso, rapier, mask, flat hat, and red-lined cape. Creezy started telling me about a little boy, I don't know who it was, someone's son, I didn't get any of it, who'd had scarlet fever and needed cheering up. Zorro was just the thing. She had to buy it. We pushed at the door. But it was one o'clock in the morning.

"My Creezy, it's one o'clock in the morning. The store is closed." Creezy wasn't having any of that.

"What do they think they're doing? Are they in business or aren't they? Closed! It's incredible! What a system! In Las Vegas the stores stay open all night. Ring the bell. Where's the bell?"

There was no bell.

"No bell! Supposing it was an emergency?"

"My Creezy, it's a toy store. It's one o'clock in the morning. We'll buy it tomorrow."

"We're not coming back all this way just for a Zorro outfit. I'll go to a department store."

But I knew already that, for Creezy, tomorrow would be

too late. Tomorrow both Zorro and the little boy would have disappeared, erased from memory. Zorro was now. She flounced away. The heels of her boots rang on the pavement. We drove off. In rapid succession the ramp, the road, and the intersection slipped by beneath our wheels. Motionless, we raced through the night. Past the trees, mown down as if by a karate chop. Only the snarl of the engine, the pallid light, the road, the buildings rushing toward us. We were riding through the sky. We were riding through the sea. Keeping one hand on the wheel and gripping the back of my neck with the other, Creezy kissed me wildly. Then suddenly she turned right, tires screaming, and drove straight at a black rectangle. I shouted, "Hey!" Somehow, by means of some contrivance, pads in the road or an electronic eye, the black rectangle gave way to a harsh light in our faces, the car plunged down a slope, and we were in the garage of Creezy's building.

five

Then came four days. Four days with just the two of us shut up in that box without going out, fed and protected by Snow. Four days between those four walls with the giant Creezys bearing down on us from all sides, closing in on us like huge, carnivorous flowers. Four identical days which ultimately became one single day, with a single flow, like a river, like casting a block of steel or cement or concrete, the sun beating against the window wall, flattened against the glass like a jellyfish, darkness clinging to the window wall like a leech, and Creezy and I immersed, welded to one another, poured into one another, crawling toward one another across the slate-gray carpet, entwined, intertwined, twin initials, her body blending with mine, her body being mine, her pleasure mine, I her, she me, she smelling of wax, sawdust, sandalwood, I smelling of wax, sawdust, sandalwood. At one point she was sitting on me, upright, her neck erect like a bird of paradise. I turned her over, the house of cards collapsed, the room spun, the posters tilted, I entered her, her heels beat the carpet, she gave her short, gasping grunt. Our cries rang out in the same second. And her eyes came back to mine like a lazy tide, like a dawdling lighthouse beam, her wide, green eyes, full of amazement.

"Where are you, my Creezy? Where are you, my baby, my happiness, my hope, my life? Where have you been?"

"I've been in you."

We went up to her room. We got into her bed. We didn't need to throw the cushions to each other any more. Snow made the bed now. She laid out my pajamas and Creezy's nightgown. One evening she even arranged them in such a way that the sleeve of my pajama jacket was curled around the nightgown. I'd never have believed that of Snow. But then what did I know of Snow? On the little bedside table was a collection of boxes and bottles containing all the stuff Creezy used continually, at night to put herself to sleep and in the morning to wake her up again. The first night I took all of them away and hid them in one of the drawers of the filing cabinet. Creezy didn't need them any more. Soon after midnight she would sink into sleep as if falling through a trap door into a pit. One night I tried to wake her up. Hopeless. Beside me lay nothing but a block of silence, a wedge of darkness. But her arm lay across my chest, her hand clutching my shoulder. One night she snored. The next morning I told her so. I shouldn't have. She gave me the cold shoulder for a full half hour, and when we made love she remained tense, her body stiffened and tensed toward a pleasure which did not come. I had cracked the present, cracked the frozen film of the moment. But at the time I didn't understand.

The flow of our days resumed, the lazy whirlpool of our hours. The record player was going nonstop. We played the same records twenty times, fifty times, until we loathed them, the thunder of drums, the wailing of strings, the American voices, "Little John," "Oh, Jericho," "Oh, Sweetheart," "And You Alone," "Gold River," "My Love," the same tunes, the same rhythms, the two of us in that box, the two of us between those four walls, hardly moving, our limbs all sticky, the taste of our bodies everywhere. Creezy made up her own words to one of the tunes and sang them all the time: goody goody goody nighttime, goody nighttime. Over and over again, shouting them out as she came down the stairs: goody goody nighttime. And Snow sang them too in the kitchen or when she brought our food: goody goody nighttime. And as she passed she gave me a lusty smile. Had Snow adopted me, I wondered. It seemed so. Did she love me? But who, in that box, in that empty space, perched on that cliff top, who was loving whom? Four days. Creezy tried on dresses, pants, boots. From down below I watched her at her dressing-table mirror. Back and forth she walked, twisting her body to look at her back. Then she came down: "What do you think of it?" I opened zippers, I closed zippers. She tried on wigs. One of them was made of pearls, nothing but pearls, all over her head. She laughed, went back upstairs and matched her pearl wig with a dress that was also nothing but pearls. I took her in my arms. There was a grinding noise and my hands could get no hold.

During those four days Creezy had no modeling sessions. Or rather she had had some but had canceled them. My work I had pushed right into the background, far away from those days. I had taken with me a report of the Finance Committee. In the margins are the scores of a game of rummy we played one evening. On one of those days, though, I did remember that an announcement which I'd recorded earlier was due to be shown on television. When it was time I turned on the set. We sat down on the slate-gray carpet. Creezy had taken a few cushions from her bed. Yes, that was certainly my name they were announcing, and then I came on. There I was in front of us, looking very serious in a collar and tie. But Creezy had slid down beside me. Creezy was nibbling my mouth. I took her in my arms. Slowly we sank down on the slate-gray carpet.

On the little screen I was still talking. I said things like "the fiscal deadlock." I said, "France has reached a turning point." My voice filled our ears. But my mouth was in Creezy's mouth, I was lying on Creezy, Creezy in the sea spray, Creezy in banana-colored bermudas, Creezy of the Bahamas. Her body, my voice, her mouth. I'd turned the sound up too high. My voice was everywhere, invading the whole room, pushing back the emptiness as it went. I was shouting as I had shouted the day of the debate on the motion of censure. Colette Dubois had given me some advice: "You want to start very quiet, not quite whispering but almost, and then suddenly you give them everything you've got." I'd done so. I'd noticed the Prime Minister looking at me under his heavy eyebrows from the Government bench, as much as to say, "What's got into them at Morlan nowadays?"

At one point I looked up. At the far end of the room, leaning in the hall doorway, arms crossed over her housecoat with the military collar, Snow stood watching me. Watching me on the screen. Her gaze went over us, over the intertwined initials on the slate-gray carpet; she was watching the serious me, the me in my collar and tie, not the me sprawling disheveled among our olive-green and lettuce-green bathrobes. My voice stopped. That was it. Snow lowered her gaze to me, as if to let me know it had been good, she had found it interesting.

Creezy wasn't so pleased. "I wanted to see you!"

"Well, that's it."

"So soon?"

"I was talking for ten minutes."

She took hold of my ears. I took hold of her shoulders. Not in tenderness any more. Occasionally a sort of fury would seize Creezy. What I saw before me then was an enemy. She threw herself at me as if she wanted to destroy me. As if she was angry with me for loving her, or with herself for loving me. We struggled. She fought with all her strength. She was smiling. It was a hard smile. With defiance in it, and I even

43

wondered sometimes if there wasn't hate in it. Hate, though, which didn't last any longer than anything else: a brittle layer, gone in an instant. All of us, one day, have had to wrestle with an angel. For me that angel was Creezy. And I knew, I knew already in that instant, that I would come out of the struggle just as he did, the man in the Bible, with my hip out of joint. With that madness, the panting, the sudden jolt inside me as my heart leapt toward Creezy, toward that woman who at one moment was me and the next moment escaped me, becoming silence, a hard smile, a steel spring, a meteorite, I was already aware that I was entering a world of which I knew nothing, a world whose bright mirrors blinded me. I have never talked about my other affairs. This one pours out of me like smoke and it is everything else that has become mere appearance, outline, imposture. What do you know of me if you don't know that I've lain with Creezy, had my belly in Creezy's belly, Creezy of the Bahamas, Creezy on the slate-gray carpet?

six

On the Friday I went home.

"Had a good trip?"

"Very good."

Betty dropped the subject. There was not a shadow of suspicion on her broad face. Or none was visible. Usually my affairs represent the dark part of myself, the hidden part, secret and shadowy, from which I emerge each time into the bright light of that which has to be and which alone has the right to be. This time I felt the exact opposite. Creezy was my brightness, it was with her that I was in the light—that bed on the gallery, the window wall, the cliff, the pale sky of the Bahamas. Leaving Creezy I came back to halls and passages, I left the stage for the wings. I came home a ghost, a cardboard man. Stamped on the cardboard were my particulars: husband of Betty, two children, deputy, elected on the first ballot with 22,537 votes. Nothing of that was entirely real any more. Or rather it had all grown dim. I had returned not from a lovers' meeting but from a trip. On a trip too you are in the light, hurried up gangplanks, met at airports, greeted in hotel lobbies. You come home and you unpack yourself the way you unpack your bags.

I went into my study. There was a stack of mail. I felt as if each letter was about to jump on me, grab me back, ensnare me again. My duties, my principles, my responsibilities, my appointments. I finally opened them. When the envelopes were all torn open, the trash sorted out, and the prospectuses thrown in the wastepaper basket, there was hardly anything left. You think your life amounts to something, and you find this is all it is: six letters, four bills, and a statement of account. Laboriously I set about answering them. My secretary wasn't there. I could have used the dictating machine. Or put everything off until Monday. I didn't. I answered them myself. Typing with two fingers. I needed that imposition. I placed that imposition between me and myself.

At about six o'clock we left. We were going to stay in the country for the weekend, with Colette Dubois. Back on the parkway. The same one I'd been on with Creezy. I didn't recognize anything. At one point, forgetting myself completely, I put my foot down hard. As if it had been Creezy driving. Betty said, "Are you crazy?" The speedometer needle fell and as it fell, something inside me went out. Antoine and Coralie were arguing in the back seat. I heard nothing. "Be quiet," Betty said. "You'll distract Daddy." Distract? Luckily Antoine started asking me questions about the French Revolution. They were studying it at school and there were a few things he didn't understand. I explained them to him, and as I did so Danton and Saint-Just were actually there, filling the whole car, banishing everything else.

My bedroom had a sloping ceiling, pink wallpaper, a pink dressing table, pink glass vases. The next day we had a barbecue in the garden. The children played croquet. I sat in a deck chair that was covered with rough canvas with pink and black stripes. Colette's husband brought me a drink. He's a writer, a playwright, the serious kind, bald and a ready talker, with a permanent chip on his shoulder. I discussed with him the crisis facing the theater. It had come up recently at the meeting of the Finance Committee. Was it really the entertainment tax that was ruining the theater? Wasn't it rather the fees demanded by leading actors? The Finance Committee had been given some figures. Colette's husband didn't have much to say about leading actors. He preferred actors with Scandinavian names who performed in costumes made of sackcloth.

Colette interrupted. She had her opinion on the subject. "This business of leading players' fees is a lot of garbage. Usually we're on a percentage. We only get expensive if the play's a success."

But the words drifted past like smoke, or like cartoon bubbles. I saw them, I saw the mouths that uttered them, but I heard nothing or what I heard meant nothing. The words rambled on, unconnected with reality. At one point Colette even paused between two remarks about the actors' union and gave me a puzzled look. She has an unusual face, sharp and pointed, with straw-colored hair. Once, a long time ago . . . I tried to pin down a memory. It was there in outline for a second, then it disappeared. Creezy dispersed it, and the memory was already no more than the foam beneath her water skis. Everything else, too, was like cotton candy, and despite my efforts it persisted in unraveling itself. The white house, the thatched roof, the green shutters, the clumps of rhododendron, the pink and blue hydrangeas, the meadow with its white railings, the little hog-backed bridge covered with ivy— the whole scene made me feel superfluous, as if I were only a silhouette placed there by an architect to enliven his model or indicate the scale. I heard Colette saying, "I've always dreamed of having a house in the country." It was only a dream, then, its very banality proved it, and it would perhaps need only a shout or a shrug of the shoulders to dispel it. It is true the sun was weak that day, giving an impression of coolness, but for me everything was cold, frozen.

And false. I could hear Betty praising this and admiring that. She didn't mean a word of what she was saying, she only likes our old house at Morlan. I watched Colette's husband. His crew neck sweater and blue linen trousers did nothing to hide the gray suit and tie to which his whole being so obviously aspired. And myself. I was the worst. Sitting in my pink and black deck chair. Barely present in the middle of all that emptiness. Think of a criminal who has to provide himself with an alibi. From ten till midnight he goes to a bar, chats with the landlord, the bartender, the old tart breathing heavily into her *diabolo menthe,* he gets himself noticed, buys a round of drinks, plays a game of cards. None of it is real. His words, his hospitality, his queen of hearts, all cardboard, a cardboard set hurriedly thrown up to hide the truth about him. The truth which is somewhere else, a strangled cry in the night, a suitcase at the airport, a blowtorch ripping the guts out of a strong room. That's where he is, not in the bar where he studiously notes that the walls are blue and the lampshades lilac. I too was somewhere else. I was with Creezy. I was an initial on a slate-gray carpet. A little girl was standing in front of me. She was talking to me. I heard nothing. Yet she was my little girl. My Coralie, my honey, my precious, my happiness, my little daughter. Only the night before I would have woken up with a start if she had so much as sighed in her sleep. And I didn't even hear what she was saying to me. I was too far away. I mean I had moved too far away. I wanted to hold out my arms to the others. Nothing moved. Beneath the pale sun nothing moved. It was only a stage set. There were no rooms behind the façade of the house. No meadow beyond the railings.

I looked at the barbecue. Just above it was a zone where, because of the heat, the air was hazy and danced about. I saw Creezy, dressed in turquoise pants. I saw the poster: spend your spare time wisely, buy a cottage in the country. In the background was a swimming pool. The swimming pool was my own addition. The Dubois don't have a swimming pool. They had been talking about it during dinner the previous evening. Colette was anxious to have one but her husband raised objection after objection: the upkeep, the filtering plant, the cost, etc. In Creezy's poster there was a swimming pool. Creezy was on the diving board, wearing an orange bikini. She shouted, "Let yourself go!" and dived. The water splashed up, sparkling like emeralds. Creezy came out. She was laughing. I handed her a glass. The ice cubes clinked in my glass. I drank. I was drinking my alibi. Colette laughed. Betty smiled indulgently.

Coralie came up to me. She was crying. She said the others were cheating and they teased her because she was the smallest. I took her mallet. I said, "I'll play a shot for you." I asked the others, "Do you mind if I play a shot for her?"

Antoine shrugged: "You're even worse than she is."

It was my turn. I played an amazingly good shot. "Well done!" said Colette. Coralie cheered up. She took her mallet back. For a second, under that pale sun, there had been something real—Coralie's face. And that ball going through the wicket.

seven

After the storm, I thought, there must come a period of calm. On the Sunday, back from the country and with the children put to bed, the Dubois joined us at home for a last drink. It turned into several last drinks. It was after midnight. The telephone rang. It stood on a low table in the middle of the room.

"This late?" said Betty, surprised.

Colette was already flapping. "It's for me. It's Nanny. Something's happened to the children."

Her husband said, "Don't let's panic, shall we?" It was his catch phrase. Always, in a restaurant, when they were ordering: "Don't let's panic, shall we?"

I picked up the receiver. It was Creezy. Her voice was no more than a mumble. She was scared. I must come right away, she said. I could hear her sobbing. "I'm all alone. I need you," came her voice out of the blackness. The blackness of night. The blackness of the ebonite. Three pairs of eyes watching me. Colette's anxious face tensed toward me. I felt hunted. Savaged.

If there'd been no one but Betty there I know what I would have done. I'd have yelled what was necessary down the ebonite, I'd have yelled what was necessary to Betty, I'd have leapt into my car and I'd have come rushing to save you, my little drowning girl, my Ophelia, I'd have come rushing to drag you from the night that made you afraid. I could have told Betty everything. But with the other two staring at me I couldn't. Did you hear me, my Creezy? I was shouting down the phone, "I can't." I could also have assumed a nonchalant manner, said something or other into the receiver, and hung up with a remark about one's colleagues certainly having a nerve. It seemed to me, I don't know why, that that would have been even harder on Creezy. No it didn't. That was what I told Creezy the next day. At the time I simply lost all my presence of mind. I told Colette, "It's nothing." I spoke into the receiver : "It doesn't matter."

I could hear Creezy's voice again stammering, "You don't understand, you can't understand." And gently, the way I had drawn the sheet and blanket over her as I had left that night, I replaced the receiver.

I said, "Wrong number."

Betty was already talking again. Colette was puzzled. Her husband's expression was sarcastic. That meant nothing, though. He looks sarcastic when he's telling you it's a nice day. The man no one can fool. God, how he gets on my nerves. Right down to his way of greeting you with a wave of his pipe. That's how you should judge a man, by things like that, the tiniest details. He suggested calling it a day. Colette protested : "Let's go to Broche's." She was probably the only one who realized that an angel had passed among us, and was still there, between the broad, cream-colored divans, and that something had to be thrown between the angel and me, anything, even an hour in a night club. Before we left I went into my office and dialed Creezy's number. There was no answer.

We arrived at Broche's and went inside, into that huge, low, black room, into that concentrated darkness where revolving spotlights swung yellow, blue, and purple beams, into that solid block of noise, that soup of sound, where a confused mass of people reeled and pitched on the dance floor, like the cars around this plaza I'm standing in. On three walls of the room huge mirrors, also apparently black, with a black gleam, made it impossible to tell where one was, impossible to see the end of the people and the tables and the little low lamps sunk in the gloom. A fat woman I'd never seen before gave me a kiss and said I was the man for her, that my speech on the motion of censure had been faultless, just what she thought herself. She showed us to a table and sat me down so close to a heavy blond that our thighs were touching. The blond gave me a look of excruciating frankness, very obviously sizing me up. She had large, cold, blue eyes. Beneath that Cyclopean gaze I felt like a diamond under the fence's lens. But it turned out I wasn't a diamond. The Cyclopean gaze had already moved on. It took in Colette's husband and moved on even more quickly. Colette's husband quite obviously disapproved. He disapproved of everything—the heavy blond, the flashing spotlights, the confused mass on the dance floor, and, in a comprehensive sort of way, the consumer society as a whole. But Colette had been right. The noise, the throbbing darkness, the yelps of the saxophone all served to calm my anguish, and it disappeared. The surging confusion soothed me.

Except that then it happened: in the middle of the black doorway between the main room and the bar, slightly above the others' heads since the bar was on a higher level, picked out by a purple spotlight, I saw Creezy. I saw her haughty smile, her erect head, her bright eyes. The spotlight swept on. I could only see shadowy figures. The spotlight came back and paused. The man operating it must have recognized Creezy because then the spotlight didn't leave her. And from the band came a roll of the bass drum ending with a crash of the cymbals. Our four days of immersion had made me forget that Creezy was somebody everyone recognized. Even out in the country, when we had gone to that restaurant, people had suddenly started leaning over their plates and whispering. Still standing on the higher floor, Creezy smiled. She blinked in the glare of the spotlights, and I saw her golden profile as she said something to the people with her—a sensible-looking, pretty young woman with fair hair and a tall young man with a loyal face. Wherever there's a woman like Creezy, there's a tall young man with a loyal face. Then Creezy stepped down onto the dance floor and disappeared in the confused mass. I couldn't see her any more.

I became aware of the music again. I heard Colette's husband saying, "Taken in occasional small doses it's a not uninteresting spectacle." I just had time to say to myself: he's going to talk about ambiance. "The ambiance . . ." he began. The confused mass swirled around and there, face to face, right in front of us, were Creezy and the tall young man. I saw Creezy's look and entered it. It passed very rapidly over my companions and then, without in any way altering her smile, without a flicker of expression, Creezy gave me a brief nod. I got half out of my chair. I bowed.

"That's Creezy!" Colette exclaimed. "You mean you know Creezy?"

I said yes. "Yes, I know her. I sat next to her on the plane to Rome a few days ago." To Betty I added, "Remember? I told you about it."

In fact I had told her about it. Betty hadn't been particularly impressed. She turned to look and said, "Oh, is that her?"

Creezy was on the dance floor, leaning forward slightly, following the tall young man's movements with her eyes. She was wearing the thigh boots she had tried on in front of me a few days before, black leather thigh boots that were like pants and went right up to her waist, and above them a gathered jacket of some gunmetal-gray material with glints of steel.

"We chatted together," I went on. All in all I felt a sort of pride and a sort of tenderness at being able to say I had chatted with Creezy. As I turned around to pick up my drink

I saw that Colette Dubois was about to say something. Then she stopped herself. I knew what she had been going to mention—the theater. The theater where I had seen Creezy for the first time. But Colette, as the saying goes, has been brought up in the rugged school of life. She kept quiet.

After a while the confused tide of people surged back from the other side of the dance floor and, through a gap, I saw Creezy sitting at a table some way away. She was alone. Despite the eyes which were turned toward her she looked, in the midst of that crowd of people, strangely forsaken. There was something about her that suggested distress. And then at last her telephone call came back to me. Her telephone call came home to me. Sitting in my apartment with those three pairs of eyes staring at me, I had thought only of myself. There, in that noisy night club, I finally heard her voice. And in the glare of the purple spotlights I saw Creezy coming apart, and I realized that I did not know Creezy. Behind her haughty profile and her air of confidence a different Creezy appeared, a Creezy who was afraid in the night and had called me up, had needed me. And who, not finding me, had immediately looked for something else, had called some friends, and had come there to find refuge in the noise. I became aware of the fact that something was being offered to me, something which, if I didn't accept it, would one day be taken from me.

Betty leaned toward me and said, "She's all by herself and she looks so sad—you should ask her to dance."

I said, "Do you think so?"

"Hey!" said Colette's husband, "You met on a plane so maybe you'll take off again."

Fool. I went over to Creezy. Walking toward Creezy through that gap it was as if, suddenly, there was no one else there and the band had stopped playing. I advanced into the silence. I advanced into the desert. Creezy saw me. She stood up. She smiled radiantly at the man sitting next to her, whom she had to disturb to get out. He leapt to his feet, knocking over his glass and catching it again. We walked toward each other through the gap. She stopped a foot away from me and immediately, without saying a word, she moved one shoulder forward and began her dance. Began to live her dance. Arms raised at right angles, head bent, eyes on the ground as if tracing with her light steps on the black slate floor a message which she herself was surprised to see there. Then she looked up. Her eyes were on me. I asked, "What was wrong this evening?" This evening? Her wide green eyes did not change their expression. It was as if she'd forgotten. I believe she had forgotten. She was living her present moment. For her, the present moment was the dance. Hands fluttering like birds, she stood pinned between her steps, imprisoned in the hieroglyphs traced by her black leather legs. And gradually, for me too, nothing else mattered. Nothing but that face lifted toward me, that gaze riveted to mine, that painted smile, nothing but the storm of the drums, the yelps of the saxophone, and the monotonous strident wail of the electric guitars. Surrounded by that thunder, deep in that cave, in that tunnel of noise, eighteen inches apart, linked only by that rhythm, we were more alone and as closely and intimately bound together as in her bed. At one point my arm brushed against hers. She shied quickly away, then a second later twisted her body around until she was very close to me and said rapidly, "I'm sorry. I won't call you up again." The words could be taken in two senses. I know I should take them in the right sense. She added, "You can do anything with me you like."

And suddenly everything came to life. Something had happened, not only for Creezy and myself but for everyone, for the whole confused mass of people reeling and pitching around us, as if a shoal of electric eels had brushed past our legs. The whole dance floor began to seethe. It was the moment of grace, the night club's moment of grace. The spotlights whirled faster and faster. The singer jumped down from the bandstand and, holding the microphone by its lead and swinging it around his head, he screamed, he fell to his knees, he got up again, he leapt in the air, he advanced, he withdrew, and before the threatening microphone the confused mass eddied and swirled with piercing squeals. The whole thing was crazy. I was crazy. Creezy in my life, that was crazy, I knew it, it made no sense at all. But I hungered and thirsted for that madness, I needed it as much as at other times I have needed wisdom, rationality, silence. Every good thing I have ever done has been done in a state of madness. Even Betty. They all said, ''The senator's daughter? Marry you? You're mad!'' I got Betty. Even my election. ''With the deputy mayor running against you? You're mad!'' My campaign was crazy. Result: twenty-two thousand votes on the first ballot, and a crushed, bewildered, haggard deputy mayor, talking to himself like a man whose wife had left him.

The whole room was now caught up in the whirlwind. I saw Betty go past, I saw Colette go past, and to Betty I offered something of the happiness I felt, gave it back to her, and it wasn't only because I owed that moment of grace to Betty but also because I owed everything I was to her, owed my very ability to experience that happiness, that fever, that elation. From far off, in the flicker of the spotlights, I recognized her expression. From far off she was telling me, ''Good, you're having fun. Good, you're letting go.'' She was my life, I knew. She was the one by my side, I knew, and was aware of it in the very moment when my heart went out to Creezy, in the very moment when my heart became caught in Creezy's nimble steps. In that chaotic throng, surrounded by the storm of the drums and the howl of electric guitars, a feeling of peace seemed to come over me. In the midst of all that disorder, a calm, peaceful, and pure sense of order seemed to descend on me. My life, my happiness. My life, I thought, without which my happiness would not be what it is. My happiness without which my life would not be what it is. Could it be, I wondered, that life and happiness are not made to go hand in hand?

🦋 | *eight*

She tried, though. Difficult as the mixture was, she attempted it. I must tell about something that I understood only later. One day I arrived at her apartment for lunch a little before one o'clock. She had told me on the telephone to come early. She'd insisted, as if it was vitally important. "I've asked someone else. You don't mind?"

She always addressed me as *vous* on the telephone, I don't know why. Using her polite formulas—please do, I'd be grateful, how kind of you—like a mechanical doll, always inappropriately, which I'd tried in vain to stop her from doing. She called me *vous* in her letters, too. Recently she'd had to spend eight days in Acapulco for a new series of posters. She wrote to me eight times. Her writing was very large and rounded, like a child's. Her letters were short, but each one contained some phrase, I don't know how to put this, some phrase which was complete, or ruthless, which ruthlessly evoked the bond between us.

"No, I don't mind at all." It didn't even occur to me to ask who the other guest was. Among all the signs I am recounting here I must add one more which I hasten to include because soon it will no longer be true: Creezy's life, I mean everything in her life that was not me, didn't interest me. Or I refused to let it interest me. I did not ask her who the other guest was for the same reason that, after the evening at the night club, I hadn't asked her who the tall young man and the fair-haired young woman were. I told myself I was being discreet. The truth was I needed to suppress the anguish I felt each time I left Creezy's company, and I could do that only by believing in a Creezy who was reduced to her simplest elements. The Creezy of the posters and the glossy magazines, the Creezy who was greeted by a roll of the drums when she entered a night club, the Creezy of steel who up until then had been able to live without me—I needed to be able to arrange all that under the comfortable heading "Creezy's Professional Life," needed to believe that everything she did without me, and I without her, took place in parentheses where nothing happened that could affect us or even matter to us.

Yet there was no shortage of warnings. That telephone call in the night, that moment when, among the flashing mirrors and the tomtoms beating out "Oh, Jericho, Jericho," I had seen my Creezy come apart and another emerge whose whole being cried out to me for help, letting me know she wouldn't always wait for me. There was that day, too, when I went with Creezy to a modeling session in the Rue des Acacias. The studio was an enormous cube of concrete and glass. Contrasting with the rough walls were parts of various sets, themselves arranged with the most meticulous attention to detail, a dining recess, a bathroom, a reading nook, emphasizing the emptiness of the rest. There a photographer, hardly saying a word, his eyes elsewhere or withdrawn inside himself, upsetting things all over the place, made Creezy sit down not on a chair but on the back of it, made her climb a ladder, rolled her up in a huge sheet of green paper with only her head showing, then made her stick her leg through a hole in the green paper, then put her inside a bright red hoop, then made her take up a yoga position, then arranged a lot of steel strips around her, then gave her a teddy bear to hold, then got tired of the teddy bear and exchanged it for a pneumatic drill, then hung up a mobile, then switched on his floodlights one after another, projecting colossal Creezys onto the ceiling and around the walls. In order to photograph her he lay down on the floor, crawled across the concrete, clambered on top of a couple of boxes, leaned over backwards, twisted this way and that, even bent down and took pictures through his legs, all the while barking instructions which were as incomprehensible to me as the incantations of a wizard, with his pink shirt and always that withdrawn, hollow look as if it were not him looking at all but his camera, as if the object of the look was not Creezy but the photograph he was taking of Creezy, and each time his camera clicked it was like a trap, like catching a moment in its trap, my Creezy was being caught, popped in the can. At first I watched everything with amusement. Until suddenly, in the middle of that glass and concrete cube, I was seized with anguish; until the moment when it dawned on me that that Creezy was Creezy too, another Creezy, who existed as truly as my Creezy existed but who was immersed in a world to which I was admitted only as a spectator, not as a participant; until the moment when it dawned on me that a person's professional life, for all that it is his public side, is also his secret side, the place where his deepest magic finds its function and where passion can sate itself as much as if not more than in love. I used the word "wizard." Every job—even my own—is a kind of wizardry, with its own rituals and passwords, its own language which is incomprehensible to other people. Creezy had only to lend her legs, her shoulders, her smile to be working her wizardry, to be celebrating her mass, to be another Creezy who was nonetheless real, who was getting on with her work, and who, in fifteen minutes' time, the session over, would no longer be exactly the same as when, arriving at the studio, she had turned toward me, smiled, picked up her bag and opened the car door.

But that warning, like the others, suffered the fate of most warnings: noticed but half ignored, heard but forgotten. A moment's happiness supervenes and the warning disappears. Or perhaps it was the same with Creezy as with me; perhaps that reserve, that shrinking back, was simply a part of our natures. Creezy never asked me any questions either about my life apart from her. She never mentioned Betty, or my children, or my work. Or was she waiting for me to mention them first? At that time there was an inhuman quality about our relationship; it had no roots, no soil even; it had no yesterday and no tomorrow; it was confined to the moment, confined to that parched fever that thrust us together. It was as if we had to be together to begin to exist; as if we emerged each time not so much from the darkness as from some undefined universe, from nothingness, to meet in a ring, raised up, and not so much to love each other as to confront each other. It was as if this very inhumanity was what we needed, as if it reassured us or fascinated us, as if in it we were in our element, or even as if we wanted at all costs to put off the moment which we knew perfectly well or which we felt would come, when everything would become more serious and perhaps painful.

On the telephone she added, "I've got to go out. I must have some flowers for my table."

Why mention flowers to me? I got it. "Don't worry. That's my job. I'll have some flowers sent to you."

I thought she'd make some protestation of pleasure. She didn't. She said, "I'd be grateful."

When I arrived at her apartment I nearly gave a cry of amazement. The living area glittered like the deck of an admiral's flagship. My Egyptian queen had become transformed into a housewife. Well, almost. Together with Snow she walked around checking each place at the table, stood back and studied the whole, went over to the flowers and rearranged them. Not knowing exactly what she wanted I had

60

sent several kinds—roses, gladioli, and three little bunches of wild flowers. The gladioli were against the window wall, two of the little bunches were on the table and the third on top of the television set. Once again Creezy crossed the room with her model's walk. Then she said, "I've got to change. I'm going up to my room. Will you look after the lady if she arrives? Please."

The lady arrived. I recognized her. It was the woman with the build of a sergeant who had been directing the photographic session in front of the Admiralty a few days before. She was a big woman with shoulders like a wrestler, thick black eyebrows, and severe protruding eyes. And a rasping voice. Following Creezy's instructions I made her welcome and begged her to excuse Creezy: she had been working, she had only just got in, and she wasn't quite ready yet. I gave her a drink. At one point, when the sergeant had her back to the gallery, I looked up. Creezy was there. She had changed. But she wasn't coming down. She was watching us.

Eventually she did come down, and started saying strange things, I mean things which weren't like her at all. She said, "I see that Jacques has already done you the honors of the house." Or "There's no need for me to introduce you two, I suppose?" "No, no," said the sergeant-woman, of whose name and occupation I was still in complete ignorance. I assumed she had something to do with public relations. Or was the director of a fashion house. She had the mannerisms of one. And the handbag. A serious-looking handbag that probably contained three appointment books and twenty contracts for every lipstick.

We sat down at the table. Snow had changed as well. She was wearing a white apron trimmed with lace. It suited her even less than the oilcloth housecoat with the military collar. For a while I suspected a trap. The big woman was surely going to ask me to do something for her, some favor, a bit of string pulling or lobbying at some ministry. Probably she had asked Creezy to arrange this meeting, and probably Creezy had seen no harm in it. I wasn't annoyed with her about it but I resolved to give her a bawling out. I was the deputy for Morlan. It was none of my business to get involved in the problems of Paris fashion houses.

But nothing happened. The sergeant-woman talked a lot. She had decided views. She mentioned the latest production at the Opera: "Worthless. Should have been cut. They didn't." She mentioned an American director: "I told him, 'Darling . . .'" None of it sounded like a prelude to a bit of scheming. At one point the conversation touched on the problems of advertising on television. This is it, I said to myself. But she was already on to something else. I finally decided the big woman had pretty good taste. Good taste couched in bad language. I said sergeant but I think I should promote her: she was more the colonel type. I recognized the breed—countess turned businesswoman—and I was hardly surprised to learn from something she said that she was related to the Bourbon-Bragances. There was a soufflé for dessert. The colonel congratulated Snow on it: "Well done, my dear." And for Creezy's benefit she added, "Pretty bright, your Spanish woman."

And there was something else. As we got up from the table the colonel-woman cast an eye over the flowers—the roses, the gladioli, and the three bunches of wild flowers. "So many flowers!"

At which Creezy said something that staggered me. She took my hand, brushed it against her cheek, and said, "Jacques spoils me terribly." She said that! She who was always so haughty, who was pride personified, who was made of steel, my painted idol, had suddenly turned into a turtle-dove. Even the colonel-woman was surprised, and in her protruding eyes, in her shrewd, dealer-countess's gaze, I caught something which expressed both regard for me and pity for Creezy.

After coffee the colonel left. We both escorted her to the elevator, Creezy leaning on my arm—the last view the colonel had of us before the door closed. Then Creezy's face, which up till then had been so animated, immediately went blank. She threw herself down on the narrow divan. "What a drag!"

"No, why do you say that?"

"Really? You weren't too bored?"

"Not at all. The woman definitely has her picturesque side." One by one I ran through the countess's vigorous turns of phrase. Creezy laughed. I said, "She's our first guest." Creezy threw herself into my arms. I realize—but only now—that that meal was a kind of dolls' dinner party. Like little girls have who want at least to pretend they're really living. I realize now that the colonel-woman didn't really matter; she was only there because the dinner party had to have a witness, like someone pressed into service on the steps of the registry office, someone who is indispensable but whom you get rid of immediately afterward. I realize now that Creezy was simply trying to live, making an attempt to bring our love into her life. I realize that now. Now that it's too late.

And another thing I know now is the reason, one of the reasons for Creezy's malady, for her anguish, her moodiness (and probably at the same time the reason for my reserve, because there I could do nothing for her). It was the twilight malady, the malady of that hour between sunset and darkness when the air seems full of wild beasts that devour the soul, that hour when, as the sky darkens, something darkens our hearts as well. Night, like a shadow, like a threat, steals over the world. For other people, for me, what has gone before is still there and carries us through: I'm at a meeting of the Finance Committee, say, I come out of the meeting with a bundle of papers under my arm and the murmur of words still in my ears, I'm thinking about what I'm going to say at the next meeting, I go home, Betty starts talking to me, Antoine comes and shows me his homework, Coralie wants to be cuddled, there are letters to be answered, my secretary is humming at her desk. And it is night; I have got there without even noticing. But for Creezy there was none of this commotion; there was only silence. The moments that had gone before did not carry her through. For Creezy the moment was no more than a moment. It didn't last. As soon as it was over it faded. All day long she had had her moments, one after another, brimful, uninterrupted, her modeling sessions, her fitting sessions, her sessions with the hairdresser—or with me—a continuous bustle of activity bearing her up, keeping her at the surface of herself. Posing for photographs, pirouetting before mirrors, sitting under the hair drier, her hair in those yellow and pink curlers that made her look more like an icon than ever. Whenever she had time she jumped into her car, tore off to Toussus-le-Noble, jumped into a plane and climbed into the sky. She had a pilot's license and it wasn't just a first- or second-stage license but a third-stage, the one which means you can make longer trips. She took me up once. My Creezy in the sky, my Creezy sitting motionless in front of me in her Plexiglas bubble, surrounded by the regular, droning roar of the engine. Below us, checkered fields, yellow and brown squares, a suburban village with its serried rows of houses, a broad expanse of water lined with yellow banks, a château with a lawn in front, roads with tiny cars gliding along them. Creezy landed the plane. She removed her helmet. She laughed. She shook out her hair.

If she had less time to spare she went riding in the forest of Saint-Germain. One day I went to meet her there. I saw her coming toward me from the far end of a path that was streaked with broad sunbeams. She halted in front of me. Her horse reared up. For a moment I saw Creezy high above me, with her haughty smile and her hair fanned out against the sky, and between me and her that great damp chest and those hoofs beating the air. I said, "What a poster!"

Creezy assumed her most professional expression to reply, "They've done surveys. Horses are a dead loss for advertising purposes."

But there comes a time when horses and hairdressers alike
are ready for sleep. And there came a time when Creezy, her
list of appointments exhausted, the bubbles of her moments
burst, went home, home to her apartment that was like an
airport; a time when she sat on her bed and wavered between
the desert ahead of her and the gadget I'd given her which
sprang open when you pressed a letter and offered you a
name, an address and a telephone number. A number that
would answer. That wouldn't say, "It's nothing. Wrong number." That would say on the contrary, "Creezy! How marvelous! Yes, of course! What do you mean! I'm going to take you
out to dinner, I'm going to take you to the movies, and then
I'm going to take you dancing." A number that wasn't mine.
I couldn't. I had my wife, my house, my children, my official
dinners. Or I could only occasionally and then not at the time
she called, at the time she needed me, when the anguish was at
its most excruciating. Then almost any bachelor had the ad-
vantage over me. He was there. I wasn't there. He could
answer. I couldn't. It's the malady of lovers. The malady of
women who live alone. A mediocre, even laughable malady,
but what difference does that make if it hurts all the same?
And there was this too: some numbers Creezy no longer
wanted to dial, or, on the other hand, the person who answered said he was very sorry but he wasn't free, he had a
prior engagement. Up until then, at a summons from Creezy,
all other engagements had been brushed aside. Now Creezy
watched as the no-man's land of the attached woman settled in
around her. A mysterious tomtom warned the bachelors off.
Let them know that dinner would be eaten without hope, the
movies would lead to nothing, and the dance would end with a
smile at the door of the elevator. Only the dedicated ones were
left. Only the tall young man with the loyal face. In the
middle of a city that had her picture up all over it, Creezy was
alone. I don't think she was ever an easy girl. If not her
principles her haughty manner, her quick temper, even her

nervousness, would all have prevented it. But it must certainly have happened that she took a man home with her on the impulse of the moment or so as not to have her bed empty. My father had a thing which he used to quote and which never failed to make him chuckle: "He went into his room and saw the bed empty. His heart did likewise." He claimed he'd read it in a novel. But the words contain a mysterious truth. An empty bed really does have that effect. Our love had even further isolated Creezy. She sat there, in front of her telephone, my little gadget bursting with numbers beside it, and she was like an empress abandoned. Snow was in the kitchen. But what good was Snow? I would be in my office. A magazine lay on the table. It opened by itself at the page I was looking for, with an enormous photograph of Creezy wearing an evening gown of iridescent blue and covered with jewelry. More than two billion francs' worth, according to the caption. On loan, of course. On loan from the French Jewelers' Association. The picture was in profile. Creezy was looking into the distance. Creezy, my Creezy, my little drowning girl in an evening gown, my little drowning girl covered with brooches and bracelets that clung like strands of weed, like dragonflies, my little drowning girl in a pool of emeralds, did you not know I was watching over you even when I wasn't there? She didn't know. Was it not enough for you that that afternoon my belly had been in your belly, my mouth in your mouth, my soul inside your soul? It was not enough. For Creezy nothing of the afternoon was left. All that was left was that enormous room, like an airport, a cube of light shining out into the night, empty, uninhabited. Where was your soul, my Creezy? Hadn't it disappeared—sucked into your posters, gnawed away by the hum of the hair drier, scattered by bursting flashbulbs? Did you still have a soul, my Creezy, or were you no more than that ravishing package—a body, a haughty smile, two billion francs' worth of jewels and a few frayed nerves?

nine

Three months ago, if I'd been asked to do something, anything, that would take up fifteen minutes a day, I'd have
exclaimed, "Fifteen minutes! With the life I lead where do
you think I'm going to find fifteen minutes?" And it was
true: I didn't have a minute to myself. Yet I found whole
hours for Creezy. I would call in to see her in the morning.
Often I found her still drowsy, struggling out of the mists of
sleep or caught in a cocoon which, gradually, layer by layer, I
peeled away. Other times I arrived in the middle of a fitting
session, with dresses thrown everywhere, cardboard boxes
lying open, Creezy at her mirror attended by an apprentice
whose mouth bristled with pins, the colonel-woman blinking
away the smoke of her cigarillo or a designer sporting gold
chains around his wrists and muttering viciously at a bevy of
female assistants. Or else I went to meet Creezy at her hairdresser's around two o'clock. I watched the man give the
finishing touches—a final clip of the scissors, a flick of the
comb, a breath of lacquer—then step back to take one last look

at his work before walking away, humble enough not to stay for the applause. I entered that imperturbable universe of murmuring activity in which each person, the hairdresser, the designer, the colonel-woman, took him or herself for Napoleon, adopting the same movements, throwing the shoulders well back, screwing up the eyes and walking with a strut. We went out to lunch. We went back to the apartment, to the room in the gallery. During the afternoon, in the May sunshine, still cold and thin at times, at other times making the window wall blaze with light, pleasure became something forbidden, something furtive; we felt we were stealing it from others and that, if they knew, there would be an outcry.

At the beginning I had told Creezy I was hardly ever free in the evenings. By this time I was spending at least two evenings a week with her. I wanted whole nights with her; I had them. I discovered, thanks to Creezy, that time is elastic, like the colonel-woman's big handbag into which, however much it bulged, she always managed to cram yet another appointment book, yet another cardigan. There were in my life certain affairs which seemed to me of capital importance. I neglected them; nothing happened. Certain letters I felt I absolutely had to answer. I didn't answer them; it made no difference. We all of us deck ourselves out with duties which one day, at a shrug of the shoulders, drop off us and disappear.

Once when Creezy was late and Snow had gone out I had to wait for a few minutes out on the landing. Creezy was indignant. Two days later she told me, "I've had a key made for you. Here it is." She said it very quickly, and from her rapid, almost mumbled articulation, from the gaze which she leveled at me, and from the stubborn expression she had assumed, I realized that, for her, what she had said was of very great importance, and that, in giving me that key, she was entrusting both herself and her life to me.

Fairly late that evening I was on my way home from a late

session of the Assembly. All of a sudden—the second before I hadn't even been thinking of doing so—I turned left. My car began roaring toward Creezy's building as if it were beyond my control. There, just as I was about to step onto the *opus incertum* path, I hesitated for a second. It was the first time I had ever come without letting her know. I went up. I christened my key. The living area was bathed in moonlight from the window wall. It looked more than ever like a translucent cube with night all around, and on the three walls the three Creezys looked like giant fish in an aquarium. Cautiously I climbed the stairs. Creezy was there, curled up in bed. I called her name. No good. I shook her. She opened her eyes. Not for a moment did she look surprised. "You," she said, "it's you." In a very faraway voice. With her arms around me, her mouth to my mouth, her whole body clinging to mine. "I knew you'd come," she went on. She dragged me down into the abyss from which, for a second, she had emerged. She was already asleep again. She lay in my arms. Her body was warm and soft, no trace of the muscles of steel; everything about her was loosened, released, surrendered. Floating, far off and very near, on the deep waters of sleep. We stayed like that for some time. Then I gently extricated myself. I watched her sleeping. A number of bottles and tubes on the little bedside table gave me a good idea of the reason for that deep, hypnotic sleep, that swoop into the shadows. I ought to have been angry. I wasn't angry. Those tubes and bottles, lying there on the little pink marble table, were a message for me. A message of distress, a message of death—without you I can't live; without you I can't sleep; without you the ghosts come back. My Creezy, my baby, my little drowning girl, my Ophelia, there in that lunar twilight I saw everything clearly. I knew very well what I might have done for you but I couldn't do it. Do you hear me? I couldn't. I loved you but I couldn't. I was yours and yet I wasn't yours. I belonged to you but I had to go away.

Gently, I kissed her. For a second, from far away, her

hand closed around mine. She smelled of wax, sawdust, sandalwood. I whispered, "Sleep, my baby." I went back down the stairs. I looked around the living area. It seemed to me I was seeing it for the last time. In the elevator I told myself I must leave her, must break it off, and not for my sake either but for hers. I told myself I had no right, no right to take up any room in her life if I could not fill it completely. That evening she was not the Creezy of the posters, the Creezy who rode the waves. She was my baby Creezy whom I must save, whom I must protect, even against myself, even against herself. I'll tell her tomorrow, I said. I'll break it off tomorrow. Tomorrow I'll break my heart. You've had a holiday from your life. Stop it now. It's time. Go home, deputy for Morlan. Go home. Next day when I telephoned she said, "Was I dreaming? Were you here last night?" Already my resolution had gone. I went to her apartment. Where was the baby I'd held in my arms only the night before? I was back with my Creezy of steel, my haughty, tough, invulnerable Creezy, I was back with our parched and arid fever. I wondered if something of my resolution had lingered on in me without my being aware of it. At one point I thought I detected a note of anxiety in Creezy's wide, green eyes, a question. But as I left she said almost harshly, no, aggressively, "You're in a great hurry today."

That key changed something between us. The first few days I still rang the bell, out of discretion, in case she had someone with her. That made Creezy angry and it was in front of the colonel-woman that she said, "What about your key? Have you left it behind?" Then, as if to hide her feelings, she added, "It's not worth bothering Snow." Also, after the key, whenever we had arranged to meet at her apartment and she had had to go out, she made quite a point of arriving after me. And if I then went up to her she said, "No, no. Wait." She went up to her room and busied herself with I don't know what. Or rather I did finally see what she was getting at: she was setting between us a little bit of life, a little bit of everyday life, a few rituals that were enough to transform our meeting. It was no longer an appointment. She came home and she found me there. She found me there not as a lover but as the man who lived there with her, who was there because there was no earthly reason why he shouldn't be there, reading a paper, listening to a record, or talking business on the telephone. Then, in the next second, the scene having been set, she came running down the stairs, she rushed over to me, she laughed, she shook out her hair, she pushed me over backwards on the narrow divan and she said, "You bastard." Other people say, "My darling." Creezy said, "You bastard." What difference does it make if you understand one another? Snow brought in the food. She didn't look at us but she was smiling. Snow was pleased.

Another day, another night rather, lying in my arms with her knee drawn up on my stomach, Creezy told me, "Listen, I've had an idea about my income tax." She explained it to me. I told her it wouldn't hold water. "Wait there," she said. "I'll show you." She jumped out of bed, switched on the light and brought me a stack of papers. And there we sat, the two of us, on the bed, both wearing our glasses—hers were so big they made me laugh.

"My Creezy, do you earn as much as that?"

"Of course," she said.

"And do you spend it all?"

"No, what do you think! Some of it I've invested."

"Invested? What in?" I shuddered. Betty knows ten times as much as I do about that sort of thing. Which doesn't alter the fact that I still think women don't understand the first thing about money. "What have you invested it in?"

"I've got a shop."

I was thunderstruck. "A shop? You've got a shop?"

"Yes, it's in the Avenue Montaigne. You know—in that big building."

"And who manages it?"

"A man."

"Who swindles you, naturally."

"No, he doesn't," she said. "Why do you say that? He doesn't swindle me at all. I keep an eye on him." She went and got some folders and ledgers out of the green filing cabinet. As far as I could tell from a fairly cursory examination the business appeared to be excellently run and the profits, at any rate, were considerable.

"My Creezy, why did you never tell me about this before?"

"About what?"

"About your shop."

"Do you find it so interesting, then?"

It's true it wasn't particularly interesting. Still, it was strange that she'd never mentioned it before. And why that night? Why did she preface it with that remark about her income tax? It's only now that I ask myself these questions. At the time, as we sat on the bed in the dead of night, once I'd got over my astonishment I simply laughed. My Creezy, my icon, my painted idol, my bird of paradise, my baby Creezy, my Egyptian queen, my empress had an entry at the Chamber of Commerce. "My Creezy . . ." I showed her the gadget I'd brought her which gave names and telephone numbers. "Do you know where I bought this? At your shop!"

But she didn't laugh. With her most serious face, kneeling there on the bed, gazing at me through her enormous glasses, she replied, "Of course you did. I have the sole rights."

 *ten*

My days with Creezy. My life, her life. Despite everything, almost despite myself (and it may simply have been that at heart I'm still a confirmed provincial who's always on his guard), I continued to believe that Creezy's world was very different from mine, a circus world, a world of trapeze artists which, if it wasn't downright shady, was certainly weird and riddled with scheming and graft. I was way off the mark. To start with, there was her agent, a sort of musketeer character with a short beard. He was Hungarian by birth and spoke with a more than usually curious accent. After our third meeting I was forced to conclude that he showed every sign of being an extremely honest man. On one occasion, in fact, I made him insert in one of Creezy's contracts a clause providing against something he'd never have dreamed of, apparently, and so malicious that according to him he was still laughing about it three days later. Her bad language apart, the colonel-woman was really no different from the old countess who owns our house at Morlan and who comes around once a year and taps all the gutters with her walking stick.

Creezy took me to see her shop. There I met a salesgirl with a face like a farmer's wife, and the manager, a tall, gaunt man with a nose like a scimitar who seemed a first-rate sort of man. He did research into genealogy in his spare time. Hearing my name, he adopted the expression of a wine taster confronted with a new vintage and said, "There's a touch of Aveyron in that somewhere." I told him that my great-grand-father had indeed been from . . . His face lit up. "I'd have taken a bet on it."

Creezy arranged another lunch party. This time with the tall young man and the fair-haired young woman. The tall young man was an architect. He was working on a big development at Saint-Cyr-l'École. Obviously he was fascinated by Creezy, and equally obviously the fair-haired young woman had resigned herself to the situation. Besides it was clearly apparent that if Creezy had suggested he spend the night with her he would probably not have been able to make it back to his development fast enough. With him it was a different sort of passion, part admiration, part amazement, part devotion. The fair-haired young woman was right to resign herself to it. I hadn't seen her properly the other evening in the night club. She was very pretty, with a calm, confident sort of beauty. She was Creezy's best friend. She could as easily have been Betty's best friend.

My secretary, who is quite a pretty girl, always used to dress very badly. In the end I asked Creezy to take her to see the colonel-woman. The two of them went to work on her. Elizabeth was transformed. After that, every time he met her, her lover brought her a box of chocolate, and recently she'd told me with a glowing face that he'd even thrown a jealous scene. From then on, whenever she answered the telephone with a few roguish, cooing phrases, I knew right away that Creezy was on the line for me.

74

In a way, we now had a little family around us—the tall young man, the fair-haired young woman, my secretary, the colonel-woman, and the Hungarian agent. And Snow, who remained our chief witness. All that should have reassured me. No, that's not the word at all—I had no worries. Should have convinced me. I don't know why but I persisted in thinking that Creezy's life couldn't possibly always have been so simple, there must be some secret places in it. Secret places I never asked myself about, secret places I'd decided against asking myself about. One day I received an anonymous letter. It said that Creezy was a notorious lesbian and had a police record of drug addiction. I didn't believe it but—how can I put this?—I didn't not believe it either; I wasn't angry, I didn't try to find out, I didn't even mention it to Creezy. I very precisely didn't give a damn. And one night, too, a night when I was sleeping beside her, she woke up with a start and clung to me, weeping, terrified, screaming for Mommy, we must telephone Mommy immediately.

"But my Creezy!"

"Call her. Call her. This minute."

"But where is she?"

"In Los Angeles."

"My Creezy, you're not going to call Los Angeles at this time of night." (Another nonsense—in Los Angeles it must have been midday.)

At last I managed to calm her. That Mommy in Los Angeles shook me for a moment. But the next minute I had already forgotten her. I'm going to say something now which may sound a bit funny: up until then, the idea that Creezy might have a mother had never once crossed my mind.

eleven

I did something that made Creezy very happy. It happened by chance. That day I went to pick her up after one of her modeling sessions. The photographer had had the highly original idea of photographing Creezy in the Place d'Aligre. Surrounded by stalls and crates, between the covered market and the little tumbledown white building with pigeons perched all over it, there was my Creezy in green-and-turquoise-striped bermudas, my Creezy in an aluminum suit, my Creezy in a periwinkle-blue negligee—that gave them something to talk about, for I arrived to find her in the middle of a group of some fifty or eighty local inhabitants whose presence was prompted by a variety of motives. When the session was over we drove off in Creezy's car. After a modeling session, in order to unwind, Creezy needed to drive for an hour, anywhere, it didn't matter where, as long as it was at an insane speed. We were just coming into Saint-Nom-la-Bretèche when I spotted a little wood. I appealed for mercy. We had our mutual concessions. I conceded her taste for breaking the speed limit. She conceded my fondness for trees.

We walked down a path. At the end of the path was a white gate leading to a house, Louis XIV, quite small, formerly a hunting lodge, I should imagine, fairly dilapidated, with the shutters closed and an overgrown garden all around it. "Fantastic," Creezy said. For her that was really the country. She jumped over the gate. She was wearing orange pants that day and a black leather blouse with silver toggles. We ventured into the garden. Huge clumps of box formed paths that were so shady as to be almost pitch-dark. They led us to a tiny walled kitchen garden where a burly woman was watering lettuce with a green plastic hose. Creezy rushed up to her. "Oh, please let me water them." Unperturbed, the burly woman held out the hose. Creezy took it and squeezed the end with her finger and thumb and the water squirted out like a fan, speckled with sunlight.

To put a bit of a face on things I turned to the burly woman and said, "We couldn't find the bell. Someone back on the road told us the house was for rent."

Still without saying a word the burly woman went over to the faucet, turned it off ("Hey!" said Creezy. "I was watering the lettuce!") and then walked toward a low, arched door in the wall and beckoned us through. "What's happening?" asked Creezy. "Is it really for rent?"

Her face expressed such pleasure, such enthusiasm, and such longing that I said, "Let's go see."

The garden we passed into was nobly proportioned, with a spacious lawn though the grass was a foot high, huge trees, a cedar of Lebanon, and several greenhouses, though they contained nothing but tools. At the end of the garden stood a large, Norman-style brick house. The burly woman led the way. Creezy held my hand and, drunk with delight, tugged at grass stems as we went. The sight of my black and orange pirate in that derelict garden suddenly made my heart swell with tenderness. We entered the reddish house and, passing through a gloomy hall, we came to a sort of office, dingily furnished and smelling of curtains and cats, where an old man with a permanent scowl held out his left hand to shake mine.

Yes, the house was for rent. The previous tenants had left. "I had to give them their notice. They had children. I detest children. They even got into my garden, sir. Ransacked everything, sir." It was evidently his pet subject. "Sir, I'd dearly love to own a restaurant just to have the pleasure of putting up a notice saying, 'Dogs and children not admitted.'"

"Charming," said Creezy.

The old man addressed his remarks to me but he never once took his eyes off Creezy. My black and orange pirate plainly disconcerted him. His gaze wandered for a moment to a grass stem Creezy was clutching in her hand. He was no doubt wondering which of the two gardens she'd picked it in and whether he ought to get annoyed or say nothing about it. Or perhaps he was simply asking himself where he could have seen that familiar face before. "Well, do you want to take it?"

God knows, the last thing I'd been thinking of on the way to Saint-Nom-la-Bretèche was renting a house. But I looked at Creezy, saw the longing in her eyes, and knew that the unexpectedness of our decision in the matter would delight her even more than the house itself. "Is it furnished, at least?"

"Oh, fully furnished, sir." Creezy had moved a little way off, and this time the man had had his back to me completely as he spoke.

"All right. Let's have a look at it."

We went back through the big garden. The old man tried to get a lead: "Are you in the films?"

"No," Creezy said, "we're in fishing tackle."

"Ah, fishing tackle," said the old man. And added, very

fairly, "I'm afraid the fishing in this part of the world . . ."

"That's just it," said Creezy. "We get nothing but fishing all week long. On weekends we don't even want to hear it mentioned."

The little house contained five rooms, all smelling of mushrooms. You could see children had been there. Everything was scratched and chipped. The wallpaper in one of the rooms, the biggest one, was covered with Snow White's dwarfs, each one repeated heaven knows how many times. But Creezy had just discovered an oval window; she went wild with delight. A curved balcony; she was in seventh heaven. The old man was chuckling to himself in the end. He must have been thinking that a woman came in very handy in a business deal.

I said, "We'll take it."

The old man launched into the inventory. He read very fast. Creezy made him slow down. When he came to the six framed engravings, Creezy pointed out to him that there were only five and made him change it. The old man looked as if he thought business deals ought to be settled between men. He tried to pass rapidly over the matter of crockery and glasses. Relentlessly Creezy counted everything and made him put down that there were four glasses missing, that the china service was incomplete, and that there were traces of saltpeter in the stove. How could I help loving Creezy?

I wrote the old man a check and we went back to the car. We drove to Saint-Nom and Creezy marched into a paint store. She wanted some cans of white paint and some brushes.

"My Creezy, what for?"

"Those dwarfs," she said. "All those dwarfs. You mean you can stand them?"

"No," I said, "but we can get a decorator in."

"Who won't turn up for a week. I'm not having those dwarfs up there another second." Then, with that very serious, tense expression she had sometimes, she went on, "I loathe Walt Disney. When I was in the States I went around Disneyland. Do you know what? I was so ashamed I looked at my feet the whole time.''

Something in her tone of voice led me to think that the opinion and even the form of expression were no more than an echo of a remark she'd heard someone else make and which had appealed to her. That happened sometimes with Creezy—traces of another life would appear, like scales. Like a kind of snobbery. Snobbery, too, comes from being afraid.

Anyway, we took the cans of paint and went back and started painting the walls. But those dwarfs were diabolical. You'd cover them with a coat of paint and then they'd reappear, far away, half obliterated, even more formidable. It needed a second coat. By eight o'clock in the evening we'd still only painted a quarter of the two walls. I mentioned going out to dinner. Creezy flung back that it was out of the question. Then she laughed, kissed me, said, ''You bastard,'' went out of the room, and came back with a big paper bag containing enough sandwiches for a party of fifteen. We ended up making love on a mattress without any sheets, lying on a tartan blanket that Creezy had brought from the trunk of her car, surrounded by the silence of the countryside. From the walls, three-quarters of the dwarfs still stared down like little old men.

☙ | *twelve*

Was it good or was it bad for us, that house in the woods?
Good, certainly, in that, once she was through that white gate,
Creezy's malady, that lack in her, disappeared. That mood in
which, as soon as there was no pleasure or occupation to buoy
her up, all was violence, shuddering, restlessness, fear—or
that frost all around us. But then, was that really the house or
the trip we had to make to get there? For Creezy, as I said,
breaking the speed limit had its therapeutic side. Whenever I
arrived at the house and saw from a distance, through the
trees, her car parked outside, I knew I would find Creezy
similarly at rest, similarly at peace. Other times we arranged
to meet in Paris. I left my car. Creezy arrived, braked in the
space of a yard, and started off again even before I'd got the
door closed. The first few times we left our cars where the
path began. Then Creezy decided we might just as well drive
right up to the house. Hardly slowing down at all, she swerved
into the path and tore along with branches slashing the windshield. I got out. I opened the gate. The car drove past me and

the tires crunched on the gravel—we were free, the magic was working.

I wonder now whether it didn't work too much, whether it didn't work like those tranquilizers Creezy used to excess and with the same result: sending us to sleep, setting a distance between us and ourselves, making us feel safe whereas the threat was still there, making us forget that, beside each love and even inside that love, its worst enemy watches and works away, that enemy being time, time being something which never sleeps but which paws the ground, wearing things away, destructively, constructively, either way we knew nothing of it, and which suddenly confronts us one day with something we do not recognize, and from which all truth has fled. Where was our truth? We went into the room where the dwarfs were and which we'd made into our room. At the beginning Creezy had cleaned and decorated furiously. She soon got over it— and I didn't give her enough encouragement. Our cans of paint stood in the corner, and three-quarters of the dwarfs were still there on the walls. On the bed we had lavender-blue sheets and a guanaco blanket. The rest of our contribution was confined to a few leather or metal objects which stood out glaringly amid the battered furniture: a record player, a red leather toilet bag, two science-fiction-type lamps, and a mobile which only worked when it was plugged in— and we usually forgot to plug it in. We'd been shopping together for our rural outfits—blue jeans and tartan shirts. But putting a pair of blue jeans on for a couple of hours is like an actor putting on a pourpoint; it means no more than that, and our two bathrobes hanging side by side in the bathroom looked like props put there by a set designer.

Yet there were moments when that house felt real, when it became a real house. Those moments we owed to Snow. Every now and then Creezy brought her along. Snow arrived, had a look around, grumbled, complained, pointed out a window lock that didn't close properly, a faucet that was leaking, a damp stain in the porch, remarked that the flowers were rotten with blight and announced as a matter of urgency that we must get a man in to deal with everything. Suddenly, that window lock existed, that faucet existed. Snow went around with the vacuum cleaner. That humming was real, it was like a breath of air in an inanimate corpse, like a puff of wind in a sagging balloon. As she moved about, the rooms became rooms, chairs and tables became chairs and tables. Snow served us tea. That tea existed.

Snow discovered a compatriot who was caretaker in a property nearby. He was a small, dark, wizened man, very dignified, with a normally stern face but which would sometimes light up. When it did he had a smile like a child's and jabbered incomprehensibly. One day we saw Snow and him in the garden, playing hide-and-seek behind the box trees. But it was a sort of slow-motion hide-and-seek, neither of them abandoning their dignity but moving about unhurriedly with just the faintest trace of mischief on their faces. Snow's compatriot soon offered his services for the odd job that needed doing around the house. He came into our bedroom carrying his tool box. It didn't even occur to him to knock. Snow had told him to go up so up he came. He started repairing the window lock, continuing his conversation with Snow, who was in the kitchen, through the open window. Behind him, lying furtively in bed, Creezy stroked my hand. Maybe that was what having a real house was: being disturbed.

But when Snow wasn't there the house turned back into a stage set. No tea, no humming vacuum cleaner, no soul. A stage set thrown up around that bed into which, three minutes after arriving at the house, we plunged like famished wolves, all nerves and steel again, ourselves again, back in our arid universe. While Creezy finished getting dressed I went down in the garden and, for something to do, I picked up the green plastic hose and started watering the flowers. Creezy came out on the curved balcony and shouted, "Don't forget the lettuce!" A charming tableau, a pretty little picture of life à *deux*, but already it was beginning to blur.

Creezy came down. She had an appointment. She was late. So was I. The lettuce forgotten, we tore back toward Paris, she to her photographers, I to my colleagues at the Finance Committee. The tires screamed. The drivers we passed screwed their forefingers to their temples. Creezy laughed. That was our truth, to be panting, rushing, back toward our universe of robots, she to her flashbulbs, I to the rustle of papers and the drone of words. But one day we were going to have to face another truth and decide what we were going to do with ourselves. The house and its surrounding foliage hid that from us. Those brief productions shrouded us in mist.

One day, as if she felt the house must be given a chance, Creezy arranged a party there. She invited the tall young man and the fair-haired young woman to lunch. Creezy, Snow, and I set out fairly early. At Saint-Nom we stopped at the baker's and at the dairy. We also bought a barbecue. I collected some wood. It was a fine day. We were able to have lunch in the garden. Gradually, a curious alliance formed between us. On every subject, the tall man always agreed with Creezy and the fair-haired young woman always agreed with me. From time to time one of us would offer the opinion that we were badly matched and that there ought to be a rearrangement of the couples. It was fun. Such fun that they decided not to break up the party but to go out and buy something for dinner and perhaps even spend the night there. I had to get back. I had a dinner party at home. I had to leave that house which was both mine and at the same time not mine, that house for which the lease was in my name but where the festivities were going on without me. Where was the truth? It was only a mirage, a stage set, as fragile as that, a dolls' dinner party, at the mercy of the slightest intrusion from outside. And Creezy knew it as well as I did, had weighed it up the same way I had. She drove

84

me in her car until we found a taxi. She went back to her little feast. One good thing: she was enjoying herself. Enjoying herself without me.

I got home with ten minutes to spare. Coralie came into my room while I was changing. She was wearing her pink bathrobe. She wanted a story. Betty came in too. She said it was time and the guests would be arriving any minute. But I sat Coralie on my knee and told her a story. Betty sat down too. She listened to my story and, laughing, added a few details. Time was standing still. There we were, the three of us. For me, those few minutes were like taking a rest, like having a bath. Where, then, was the truth?

On another occasion, since we were still at the house at about midnight, and in bed, Creezy decided to spend the night there. And again, as I hadn't said anything at home about being away, I had to go back, and I had no alternative but to take Creezy's car. I told her I'd bring it back to her the next day. Creezy went off to sleep. Quietly, I got dressed. I set off in her car. As soon as I was on the road I was seized with misgivings. I imagined Creezy waking up, frightened or having suddenly changed her mind, and wanting to leave and not being able to. I spotted a taxi on its way back to Paris. I drew level and signaled the driver to stop. He couldn't understand what I meant. Since when did a person driving a car ever need a taxi? Keeping one hand on the wheel he checked all his doors and signaled that everything was all right. Finally he pulled up. I persuaded him, not without some difficulty, to follow me. He followed me, for some reason flashing his headlights at me, probably to convey his disgust at having to venture so far into the woods in the dead of night. I went up to the bedroom. Creezy was still asleep. In one corner, left over from our predecessors' children, stood a blackboard. I set it up beside the bed and, finding no chalk, I wrote in white paint, "Your car is downstairs." I left again with the taxi driver, who kept me under constant surveillance in his rear-view mirror all the way back to Paris. When we got there he accepted my money with deep suspicion.

The next morning I set off very early back to Saint-Nom. Everything was as I had left it. Creezy was still asleep. She opened her eyes. She said, "It's you." I got back into bed beside her. It felt as if I had been there all the time, as if my comings and goings in the night had been nothing but a dream. As if. Only as if. It wasn't so. The truth was that I hadn't been with you all night. And yet it was that same morning, in that nursery, in that room where something of childhood still lingered on, it was that same morning that Creezy said to me, "I'd like . . . I'd like to have a child by you."

thirteen

"I'd like to have a child by you." She, my Creezy, my
Egyptian queen, my painted idol, my icon, she who was so
hard, who came to me out of her frozen universe and out of
the pale sky of the Bahamas, with her helmet and her haughty
smile. And I, in the chill of the morning, freshly landed from
my night's voyage, I heard her say those words. And immediately a confused joy welled up in me. Was it possible that
everything was going to make sense at last, and that, from our
furious embraces, life might spring? My impulse was to shout
yes. But my make-up is such, unfortunately, that I believe
that the strictly honorable thing to do in all circumstances is
first of all to deal with the objections and not to give in to
impulse, and even less to give in to another person's impulse. I
put the objections to her: her life, my life, whether we even
had the right to have the child. I said, I think, what any man
would have said. I didn't see that that was just it, that at that
particular moment I could not be just any man. I didn't see
that, for Creezy, it wasn't so much an earnest of love as a last

desperate attempt to shake off the numbness that was both sublime and deadly, to jolt us out of ourselves, to join in that life which incessantly escaped us, which incessantly rejected the tinsel we decked it with, to halt at last time's noisy pursuit of us, didn't see that this was an act whose meaning lay in its very senselessness, an act which represented, for her as for me, a matter of life or death. And neither did I see, in spite of all I had learned, that I ought, in that instant, to have run to meet Creezy, run to be with her in her universe where it was the instant alone that mattered, the moment, that moment in which she had cried out to me, but which, if I didn't respond immediately, would be gone forever. I ought either to have accepted or refused but done so immediately. I didn't refuse. I said, "Think it over." I said, "Sleep on it." Yet I knew that, for Creezy, the night only brought poison, delay brought only death. Next day, when I said, "Let's have that child," her wide green eyes were expressionless. The moment had gone. We didn't have the child. But I believe it was then, starting with that child, that something between us began to come apart. And now, even now, of that love which has fled away, I am bold to say I regret only one thing—that child of yours, my Creezy.

✥ | *fourteen*

I got to her apartment at about eight o'clock. I found her in her Formica kitchen, busy preparing a salad into which she was putting pineapple, avocado pear, nuts, a mango, and some tomatoes.

"I wanted to be alone with you. I've sent Snow off to Neuilly to the movies where they show films dubbed in Spanish."

"In Spanish? At Neuilly?"

She flared up immediately. "You always doubt what I say. I telephoned to check."

The next minute her bad mood had disappeared and she was showing me a game her agent had brought her—a scaffolding framework about a foot high, in three levels, with rows of steel balls suspended from it. As soon as you lifted one ball the others began to swing rapidly to and fro, each time in a different and unexpected way, either two in one direction and three in the other, or all together, or only one, moving abruptly, producing a dry, clacking sound. Creezy got very excited and tried all the different combinations. I played too.

The thing had a magical fascination with its cold, bright, rapid, swinging motion, the regular sound it made and the fact that we couldn't crack the secret of how it worked. Creezy wanted to understand it. She couldn't understand it. That annoyed her. We ate our salad very quickly. We played faster and faster, jostling the balls, setting all the rows going together; the thing was like a metronome gone mad, like a barren, mechanical quarrel.

Then, all of a sudden, Creezy had had enough; she abandoned the steel balls and started telling me about a singer called Sammy Minelli. She had posed for the jacket of one of his records. He had a show on in Paris at the time. She had never heard him in the flesh.

I said, "We'll go sometime."

Not at all. She couldn't go another minute without hearing that singer. She went off to change. She swapped her lime-green pants for a red dress with spangles. Asked how she looked, I expressed some reservations. Usually when that happened Creezy put on another dress. Not that evening.

We arrived at the theater. I asked at the box office. Sammy Minelli was heading the bill. He had only just started. The house was packed but, seeing Creezy, a little man popped out, fussed around her, and had two seats added in one of the aisles.

The noise was terrifying. On stage, in silver pants, Sammy Minelli swung his guitar around his head, hurled it into the wings, ripped off his shirt, yelled bang bang, rolled on the floor and screamed, "Wait for you tomorrow, wait for you forever." His agonized face appeared above the footlights. Behind him three musicians were flexing their knees and grinning all over their faces. Beside me sat a blond girl, quite young, not eighteen, plump, and with her moonlike face covered with a mixture of sweat and tears, whimpering, shivering and hugging herself. Behind her an emanciated youth lurched forward in his seat, smashed his fist into his palm and shouted,

"Keep it up, Sammy! That's the stuff, Sammy! You've got it right there, Sammy!"

I looked at Creezy. Her head, her shoulders, her whole body were responding to that lunatic rhythm. She pressed against me. She said, "He's marvelous, don't you think?" Marvelous? Then, very gradually, inside me, something began to give way, and I too entered into that primitive rhythm. The delirium had reached even greater heights. Sammy Minelli threw bottles, chucked fireworks, there were explosions, thuds, flashes of light, Sammy Minelli gave a scream, there was nothing but that square mouth screaming, the audience screamed with him, it was as if the whole audience was pouring out of that square mouth. He sobbed, he writhed in agony, he yelled bang bang. Or rather, in the middle of the uproar you could see he was screaming bang bang, you couldn't hear him, the screaming itself by now was indistinguishable from the whole seething mass. The plump blond couldn't stand it any more. She slid down into the aisle and started crawling around, beating the ground with her forehead. The aisle was a mass of people. One girl was sobbing and clawing her cheeks. Another, her hair all over the place, pulled open her blouse and screamed, "Take me, Sammy!" A youth was throwing punches into thin air, giving grunts of pain. Another dropped on all fours, beating time with his head. The musicians were no longer grinning. Their movements had become jerky and convulsive. Beneath the uproar there was a dull rumbling, as in a bowling alley, as if underneath the auditorium there was an enormous bowling alley; it was like a thunderstorm, an army on the march, a raging sea.

Then, abruptly, Sammy stopped. He bowed stiffly, Prussian-style, his arms at his sides. The uproar doubled in volume, became like a huge ball, like a thick, black cloud. Sammy was still bowing. There seemed to be nothing left of him but that mechanical bow. He seemed to have lapsed back into a stiff dummy.

Creezy took my arm: "We'll go say hello to him."

An iron staircase led us down into a dimly lit courtyard where two hundred youths and girls armed with ball-point pens were jostling for position in front of a door over which a couple of men were standing guard. For Creezy, I knew, that kind of obstacle simply didn't exist. She cut a path through the mob with the greatest of ease, fending off a few of the wilder ones, and reached the guards who, without a moment's hesitation, threw open the door and stood back to let us pass. A chorus of boos followed us.

We were in a beige and black prison corridor, beige below, black up to the low ceiling. All the paint was peeling off and the only lively touch was provided by a red fire extinguisher. We found Sammy's dressing room at the end, a narrow rectangular space cluttered with mirrors, odds and ends of clothing, and telegrams pinned up on the walls. Sammy was there, stripped to the waist, attended by a frizzy-haired youth who was rubbing him down with a shocking-pink towel.

"Creezy!" said Sammy. And turning to the frizzy-haired youth he repeated, "Creezy!"

The youth, without interrupting his rubbing, gave a nod as if to say, "With a talent like yours it was a cinch!"

"O.K., cut it," said Sammy.

The other stopped rubbing and finally turned to look at us. I'd thought Sammy would be taller. In fact he was on the short side, with a frail build, a blotchy complexion, too many teeth, and hair growing down his neck.

Creezy, saying what had to be said, told him he was terrific. "Terrific," repeated the frizzy-haired youth, who turned out to have a bad stutter.

"No kidding, you liked it?" asked Sammy with an expression that made him look ten years younger. He looked a bit like a hotel page boy—innocent, wily, and deeply corrupt, all at the same time.

"Terrific," said Creezy.

"One day I'll sing just for you."

"Terrific."

"I'll come to your pad and bring my guitar."

"Terrific." By the seventh "terrific" I was beginning to get annoyed.

"The gentleman included, of course," Sammy added tactfully. He had not yet drunk his fill of compliments. He had to have mine too. "And you, sir, how did you like it?"

I said, "Terrific."

The manager of the theater arrived. I knew him vaguely. He started bellowing, "How are you, sir! I couldn't be more surprised to see you! A member of the Chamber of Deputies!"

Sammy and the frizzy-haired youth looked at me with astonishment, not unmixed with anxiety, and Creezy herself turned to me as if she had just discovered that I belonged to some strange, unheard-of breed; it was as if some kind of mysterious barrier had just sprung up, with the three of them on one side and the manager and myself on the other.

"I've got something I'd like you to see," said the manager. "No, please. You're just the man I need." He probably felt the expression was a little too familiar. "I mean you're an eminent representative of the Government." The astonishment on the faces of Sammy and the frizzy-haired youth was now complete. "I must show you this. It might interest you."

The manager led me away, back along the corridor, up a concrete staircase and along another corridor. At the end of that corridor he opened a window. He pointed out a building nearby, or a wall—from where I was standing I couldn't see whether it was just a wall or whether there was a building behind it—a huge wall, pitted with holes, scarred, cracked, held up by enormous balks of timber like gibbets, which stood out black against the black sky.

"Look at that! In the middle of Paris! Isn't it scandalous? One day that's all going to come crashing down on my nut, I mean on my premises, and I'll be manager of a heap of rubble.''

At the risk of making matters worse I told him to put his case to the City Council.

His face lit up. "Do you know the right person to approach?''

No, I didn't know the right person to approach. His face darkened. He's a fat man, the manager, with jowls like elephant's ears, and they wobble. I led the way back to the dressing room. Along the corridor, back down the concrete staircase. The manager was still hanging on. "I know those types. If you don't find the right person you don't get anywhere. Couldn't you give me the name of the right person to approach?'' I thought any minute he was going to slip me an envelope. I was very angry at being there. I was angry with Creezy for bringing me. The manager tried vainly to hold me back by grabbing my arm. I was walking so fast that he tripped in the corridor. He said, ''All right! All right!''

At last I found the dressing room. Sammy Minelli was busy buttoning his shirt. Creezy was standing in front of him, her eyes sparkling. There was nothing ambiguous about their attitude. And yet, between them, I was aware of something slimy, some kind of slimy complicity. Once again the suspicion crossed my mind that Creezy's life, her past, had some secret cellar, that there was something secret about Creezy. And the suspicion was no longer a matter of indifference to me. However, as soon as I entered the dressing room, things slowly swung around and dropped back into place. Creezy came up to me. Sammy thanked us again. The manager put on his best Punch and Judy voice to say, ''Well, then, kids?'' and without any ceremony I dragged Creezy away.

In the car she tried to joke about it. She said, "I don't think I'll take you to a concert again.''

I said curtly, ''I very much hope you won't.''

In the bedroom, standing on either side of the bed, we

began to undress. I said, "I also hope you'll never let that lout in here."

"What lout?"

"That Sammy Whoever."

She didn't look up at me. Her face was set in her stubborn expression. "I've asked him for the day after tomorrow."

"That's inconvenient. I'm not free."

"You're never free. It's his day off."

"I don't see that that's any reason to have him here."

Everything between us had turned to steel again. The words were cold as ice. To get to her dressing table Creezy passed very close to me. "Do you want me to spend my whole life waiting for you?"

"I'm not asking you to wait for me. I'm asking you not to just do the first thing that comes along."

"While you have a high old time at your dinner parties."

That was it. It landed. The flat of my hand. Violent. Brutal. Creezy stared at me, her hand on her mouth. I felt ashamed, bitterly and miserably ashamed. But at the same time, so unlike Creezy had that phrase been, so unlike my Creezy, that it felt as if I had not slapped her but someone else, another woman who lived in her, alongside my painted icon, alongside my bird of paradise, buried deep in her, someone whose existence I had long suspected but whom I thought had gone, who hadn't gone, who had just loomed up again—how? born of what? revived by what intrusion into the past? —another woman who deserved no other treatment.

I picked up my tie and put on my jacket. Creezy was already at the top of the stairs. "If you go now I'll never see you again." There was a kind of frost all over my face and hers was ugly, twisted in the dim light, all black and white like her photograph on the bottom of the table.

I stretched out my hand to push aside that woman I didn't know. She jumped and cringed back as if she was afraid. A second later her mouth was in my mouth, her body against me, clinging to mine. We rolled back onto the bed. Everything was still steel. Her body was hard beneath me and her hand on my neck was like a claw. I entered her and she shook her head from side to side and back and said, "Slap me. Slap me again." Her whole body was arched against mine. She spoke very rapidly, mumbling, the words were like froth on her lips, I didn't understand everything she said: "It was him! The bastard! Slap me! He asked me if I was happy with you. And I didn't say anything. I let him believe . . . Slap me. I should have shouted out. Shouted that I belong to you. To you. Only to you."

Her body writhed beneath mine, contracted, tensed viciously, it was full of anger, full of bitterness, she dashed her body against me with great thrusts I could barely control, her eyes shut, her head thumping the bed, rolling about; I saw her face was covered with the same film of sweat and tears I'd seen on the face of the blond girl at the theater, I had a stranger under me, crying out under my thrusts, shouting, sobbing; anger took hold of me, welled up in me, madness, anguish, all the anger in me bursting out, I lashed out wildly, lashed out not at her but at myself. I hit out, I'm hitting her, my icon, my baby, my Creezy, my bird of paradise, as if I must run to earth in her and drive out of her an enemy I hate, hate with my whole being, as if I must shove into her, ram back into her that horrible phrase that came out of the uproar in the theater, as if I must kill, kill that other woman that loomed up in her, and it's my destiny, lying there, that I'm abusing, I know it, and I hit out, my life, my happiness I'm pillaging, brutalizing, my Creezy, you're mine, swear that you're mine, yes, I'm yours, yes, utterly, yours. And Creezy, at last, gave a long drawn-out scream.

🦋 | *fifteen*

It was a paroxysm. It should have brought us closer together. Once again I felt that, with Creezy, everything that brought us closer together at the same time separated us, tore us apart. There had still been love in that furious embrace; there had also been mutual exasperation and perhaps even hatred. But there came a day when, from love, love was born, that is to say love as a third party which ruled us, and which abused us, whose face, depending on the day, was bright or dark, and without there being much we could do about it any more. There always comes a day when love becomes what people call love, that sickness, that virus, that thing which makes it said that a man has fallen in love (fallen—what an admission!), that enemy who eats us away inside. Behind my Creezy of steel I saw other Creezys loom up, the one who was afraid in the night, the one who staged around us a life which was not ours: the little house, the little family. And still those Creezys made my heart swell with tenderness. I had no tenderness, only hate, for the woman of that night of Sammy Minelli; the woman who drew up her accounts every evening and was even more meticulous with me than with the manager of her shop. A woman who draws up her accounts is a woman who thinks she's being robbed. A woman who thinks she's being robbed is a woman who is well on the way to becoming mean. If one day I stayed with Creezy for two hours and fifty minutes, the next day it was, "Yesterday you barely stayed two hours." If I happened to go a day without seeing her, it was, "I have to put up with whole days without you." If I mentioned that the heating in the little house wasn't very good, a week later it was, "You're only trying to find a way of getting rid of the place." I too started drawing up accounts. "Two hours and fifty minutes is not two hours. It's nearly three." We argued over those ten minutes like cashiers caught robbing the till. In the evenings, too, she would no longer go to sleep in my arms. Each time I left, it was an agonizing wrench. One day I got to her apartment before her and had to take a call about a modeling session she was wanted for. I opened her appointment book and found that each of my visits was recorded there with the minutest exactitude: "Arrived at four-thirty, left at seven-twenty." Probably it was merely to give a little more reality to those hours that had flown by so fast. I saw only a petty-mindedness that irritated me. I was wrong, I know. I was unjust, I know. And that was probably what exasperated me. I knew full well that, in the end, everything came back to a single obstacle, and that obstacle was me, that other life, that other home that I persisted in trying to save. And I must add, too, that for Creezy they were only moments of sudden moodiness. The next second she would be laughing, shaking out her hair, and she would throw herself into my arms, her mouth in my mouth. For me they were not moments and I dragged them around with me.

One night, when I thought she had fallen asleep, I gently slipped away, got dressed, and turned to look at her. She was sitting on the edge of her bed. And she said, "Take me with you." She said it almost under her breath, her head bent, not even looking at me, tracing something with her forefinger on the sheet. I went to her. I took her by the shoulders. She looked up. In the pale light coming from the window wall, I saw the film of tears on her face. "Take me with you." No expression in her voice, even. "Take me with you. I can't go on being all alone." She shivered. The night was all around us, and we were lost in it.

"My Creezy, my baby, I can't and you know I can't. I can't. You've got to understand that."

"Yes," she said, "but take me with you."

"I can't."

"Take me with you."

"I can't."

sixteen

Summer came. Creezy had to go to Rome for a series of photos for the French Fashion Designers' Association. She asked me to go with her. The dates were awkward. I had to drive Betty and the children down to our old house near Morlan. In the end we decided, or rather I decided—Creezy said nothing, she said, "Do whatever you like," she had on her stubborn look— I decided, then, that since in any case she'd be very busy for the first few days it would be better if I joined her when she'd finished her work and we could spend a few days at the coast. I left on a Tuesday. Creezy left on the Wednesday. The arrangement was that she should send me a telegram as soon as she arrived, telling me how long she would be tied up. On the Wednesday I spent an exquisitely enjoyable day tramping around the countryside. I found the stream where we used to fish, the old willow, and the three oak trees, one of which had been struck by lightning and completely hollowed out. Around five o'clock I was sitting in the garden with Betty. She talked. I talked. Everything was simple, ordinary. It seemed to me that I had emerged from a confused hubbub, a chaotic jumble that was a mixture of the restlessness of Paris and Creezy's own restlessness. Once again I experienced the pacifying quality of trees. Betty, the children, the countryside, all lay around me like a flowing robe. Only, that evening, there was no telegram. Nor the next day. I wanted to telephone. I couldn't. There was only one phone and that was in the hall.

On the Thursday afternoon I went into Morlan to the post office. My arrival, of course, was instantly reported. The sub-postmaster came out and started fussing around me. "I'm afraid the postmaster isn't here. He's on vacation. He will be extremely sorry to have missed your visit." He summoned the telephone superintendent.

The superintendent said, "There's a half-hour wait for Rome."

The sub-postmaster said, "You mustn't wait here. Come take a seat in my office." And added to the superintendent, "Put the call through to my office." So we went into his office. "Is your telephone out of order, then? You should have let me know."

"No, not at all, it's working perfectly. I was in town and I have an urgent call to make."

"Urgent?" The sub-postmaster buzzed the superintendent: "Tell them it's urgent."

I was on the verge of becoming very angry and my anger, very naturally, became transferred to Creezy. It was because of her that a few days before I'd had to put up with that theater manager and it was because of her that I had to put up with this sub-postmaster and his suddenly conspiratorial look. Faced with a lie, men let their true nature rise to the surface and they become hideous.

The telephone rang. The sub-postmaster got up briskly. "I'll be off," he said, "I'll leave you to it." And even before I picked up the receiver he'd tiptoed out of the room.

I asked for Creezy. A cheerful voice replied that Miss

Creezy was not there. I asked whether I could leave a message. There was a brief confabulation at the other end and then the voice came back, slightly less cheerful, to say that Miss Creezy had left the hotel and gone to another, they didn't know which one. I slammed down the receiver. The sub-postmaster came back. He can't have been far away.

I went out to my car. The best thing, probably, would have been to wait. I couldn't wait. I had to vent my anger on someone. I could only vent it on Creezy. When I got home I told Betty I'd had to move forward the date of my departure for Rome. I got up at least ten times during that night and the next day I left for Nice, driving fast. At one point, around Avignon, it occurred to me that maybe Creezy's plans had had to be changed, that she'd had to go back to Paris or that the job had taken her somewhere else, in short that I might arrive in Rome to find her gone. Too bad, I thought. Good. It suited me to think Creezy might be in the wrong. On the Esterel highway, with the needle touching a hundred, my fury subsided a little. That's one thing I've inherited from Creezy—a love of highways.

Arriving at the airport with an hour to spare before my plane left, I bought a Michelin guide and set about telephoning all the hotels in Rome, in order of size. At the third one I was told Miss Creezy had just gone out. I left a message.

I arrived in the hotel lobby to find Creezy there. The lobby was huge. She came toward me from the far end, with her model's walk, looking absurdly extravagant for the time of day in an evening gown of emerald ostrich feathers, turning heads as she came.

I said, "What happened to your telegram?"

"I didn't have time," was her answer. "I didn't think there was any hurry."

Her wide green eyes were expressionless. Was she lying? Was she trying to hide something from me? Why the change of hotels? Was it just her revenge for the disappointment I'd caused her by not going with her? All these questions flashed through my mind very quickly, and if I put them to myself at all it was without curiosity. I was suddenly indifferent to it all. My anger had been used up on the Esterel highway. All that was left in me was something crumbling, pieces of walls collapsing slowly inside me, in silence. At that precise moment —in that lobby, with the hotel porter standing a couple of yards away, a man leaning on the reception desk making a telephone call, a woman asking for something in English, Creezy in her evening gown, heads turned to stare at her—I decided to break it off.

A young man came up to Creezy. He told her it was time to go. Creezy said to me, "What did you tell them when you called? They went mad, they sent a messenger to look for me. I asked for the session to be held up so that you wouldn't arrive and not find me here. Now I must go back."

I said, "Go on, go on. I'll see you this evening."

I went up to my room. I told myself I was going to break it off. I didn't even feel sad. Breaking it off was probably the only free act still open to us—and the only act that would still be like us. I determined to break it off and at the same time I subscribed to the eternal folly of believing that it is possible to do it well. I decided to break it off but I still wanted to give Creezy those few days I'd promised her.

Creezy came back. We went out to dinner. Did she know already how I felt? We talked like a pair of convalescents. "If you like, my dear, just as you wish, my dear." On the way back to the hotel we walked down the Via Veneto, past the café terraces. As we went I saw in people's eyes the same perplexity I had experienced myself the first time I saw her, as if they were suddenly confronted with someone they had seen in a dream.

The next day Creezy had one more modeling session. I joined her there. It was in front of the Trevi Fountain. They had brought along a lemon-yellow caravan in which Creezy changed between shots. She appeared successively in an evening gown, a formal suit, a summer mink, absinthe Bermudas, and a figured dress, each time accompanied by little women with their mouths full of pins. What was I doing there, I thought, trailing after that woman who stood for everything I considered most vain and futile? The gods and sea lions of the fountain were behaving more sensibly than I was. One of the photographers stepped backwards and trod on my toe. It didn't even occur to him to say he was sorry. I was only an onlooker, someone who was in the way.

Very annoyed, I went over to Creezy and said, "I'm going back, I'll see you at the hotel."

The photographer's gaze did show a flicker of respect then. But I couldn't help wondering whether there wasn't an infinitely greater degree of complicity between Creezy and him than between Creezy and myself. My Creezy. She was my Creezy. But it was he who was going to carry her off, in his little black snare that went click.

On my way through the lobby I had a word with the hotel porter. For those few days with Creezy I wanted a very special hotel with a big garden all around and no one else there. The porter told me he'd take care of it.

I went up to my room. The telephone rang. It was the president of the Franco-Italian Section. He had just heard I was in Rome. How did he know? There had been a three-line notice in one of the papers. Might he have the pleasure of lunching with me? No, I said, thanking him, I was only passing through, we'd had a very heavy session at the Chamber and I wanted a few days' rest by the sea. By the sea? The *onorevole* made several loud exclamations. He had just what I needed, a little house the other side of Sorrento, charming, very secluded, he only used it in August, he'd be delighted to lend it to me. Delighted, really, no trouble at all. I hesitated for a second. With Creezy? One day he'd find out I'd been there with Creezy. I decided I didn't care. That too was a matter of indifference to me now. I accepted.

An hour later he was there; he'd called the caretaker and brought a map of the route. It was all clear as far as Sorrento but after that you had to know what you were doing. In his enthusiasm he even wanted to lend me his car. No, no, I told him. I'd hire one. I called the porter over. He said he'd take care of it. The car would be there the next day.

Creezy came back. "I've finished," she said.

I said, "We're leaving tomorrow."

"Terrific," said Creezy.

seventeen

The magic of geography—because we were going south I had
the impression that the highway sloped downhill, that the car
was simply rolling down it, and that it would have done so
just as well without the engine. Once out of Rome, under a
blazing sun that gave the landscape the spareness of an architect's drawing, as I swung the car around the intersections I
saw something hover above us and descend on us, like a
helicopter when it's just landing and it looks as if it is tasting
the water with its floats, I saw something descend on us that
was not exactly happiness but which was at least a sweetness, a
kind of grace. Beyond Naples the highway put on a show for
us. There were acacia trees, and creepers hung between them
like leafy curtains; cookie-sellers hailed the passing cars, and
the houses were cubes of pink, ocher, and pale blue.

At Pompeii we took a road which wound along the coast
through olive plantations and old, sun-baked villages. Creezy
said it reminded her very much of Mozambique, an island off
Mozambique which she'd visited—I didn't get the name—ex-

Spanish, a few huge pieces of dark furniture, and a tiled floor representing a naval battle—bulging sails, a sea sprite blowing a conch, an admiral in a blue cuirass, and a towering sea in which, just at the foot of our bed, could be seen the terrified faces of several drowning men. The bathroom was decorated with gilt mosaics but the gilt had gone black with age. Two copper swan-neck faucets peered down into an ancient bathtub with crocodile feet. According to Creezy the place reminded her more and more of her island off Mozambique. The next day we went into Sorrento and hired a motorboat. It had twin two-hundred horsepower engines and flat yellow cushions on the seats around the stern. They gave us a sailor, too, a lanky youth, as weather-beaten as they come, with blue eyes and the same knowing smile as Colette's husband. Creezy tried Spanish on him but his only reply was to mimic sadly what she had said, and from then on he took refuge behind his knowing smile and hardly said another word. The sea was like glass. We rounded a headland and then another one. I took the wheel. Creezy, standing beside me, holding on tightly to the windscreen, gave herself up completely to the wind and the roar of the engines. We reached a deserted spot. Not another boat in sight, massive cliffs like elephants, covered with brown stunted bushes, not a single trace of civilization except for one ancient, ruined tower and, right at the top of the mountain, the oval bowl of a radar station. I stopped the boat.

"Do you want to do some water skiing? Wait—do you know how to, though? I always thought that Bahamas poster was rigged."

"Bastard," said Creezy. "I'll show you." And as the sailor drew two skis out from under the seat she added, "Hey, that's for beginners. I use the slalom." There was a slalom too.

Creezy lowered herself into the water. I paid out the line. We started off. Creezy came out of the water. With her boyish shoulders and her legs together on the single ski she was no more than a slender, tapering triangle. On either side of her the wake of the boat formed two thick rolls of foam, but foam so powerful that it looked solid. Creezy ran up the left-hand roll, leapt into the air, and fell back onto the smooth water beyond it. Then she recrossed the roll and leapt over the other one. It was like a dance. There seemed to be no effort involved. She was surrounded with spray just as on the Bahamas poster, and the water gushed and snorted past her. Creezy leapt over the roll of the wake again. She came up almost level with us, leaning over like a yacht under the wind. She sped like an arrow, she skimmed over the surface like a gull. She glided over a sea as smooth and flat as a pewter tray, and this time it was she who was throwing up the spray, like a fan, now to the left, now to the right, depending on which way she leaned her body. The sailor went into a long turn. Creezy flew. She traced a dazzling arc across the sea. She was flying on the end of her line like a tiny little puppet. My little puppet on the sea. My little puppet in the spray. And, all around us, that desert in our image, the massive cliffs and the sun bursting like a slap on the sea. Back inside the wake of the boat, Creezy brought the two handles of the line around behind her. Standing like that, motionless in the foaming wake, elbows out, she was like an amphora. We slowed down. She let herself slide into the water. We went over to pick her up. "Your turn now," she said. My turn to furrow the sea, my turn to feel the water leaping beneath me, my turn to be that little puppet in the spray, to be held, by Creezy, on the end of a rope. And I took the plunge, we took the plunge into those eight days which, like our four-day immersion in the apartment, soon became a single day, a single flow, a single mold, hardly punctuated by the nights, dateless, timeless.

We got rid of the sailor and headed for the open sea. Creezy had taken a diving outfit out of one of her suitcases, a black garment of some shiny material, with steel buttons, ultimately no stranger than the suits she'd been modeling in the Place de la Concorde. She looked as if she were going to a party. She put on her mask and flippers, picked up her harpoon, strapped a knife to her thigh; she stopped looking as if she were going to a party. She dived and I cruised around her in the boat. Then she came up. It seemed there was no sign of any fish. She took off her equipment, keeping only the mask and flippers. "Coming in?" she said. I donned my mask, too. Creezy had disappeared. I floated face downward, looking for her. At last she showed herself. Hands down beside her body, flippers threshing softly, she emerged from an underwater crevasse twenty feet below me, a sort of corridor of rock, and passed through a rugged arch. I swam down to join her. She came up. Our bodies brushed as we passed. She came down again. The bottom was smooth at that point, covered with little white petals, like a field of daisies. My Creezy swam up toward me out of the daisies. Farther on the bottom was pink and gray, a brittle, grainy pink, a little like the tweed suit Creezy had worn that day we had lunch out in the country. Farther on still it was strewn with rocks, cracked, uneven, suggestive rather of Roman ruins. Together, our bodies occasionally touching, our only movement a faint threshing of the flippers, we glided among the Roman ruins. Where the bottom was less deep our shadows glided along beneath us, slowly, like the shadow of an airplane over the fields as it approaches the airport. In one place huge dark plants grew, like fur coats. Creezy swam up toward me out of the opossum skins. She swam up toward me through the beams of luminous blue that pierced the sea. We swam over a fairly large flat rock, only a foot or so beneath us, covered with a lime-green, mossy growth, and then immediately, suddenly, it fell away to emptiness, an apparently bottomless abyss where the blue of the water turned to black, and it was as if we had taken off and were flying, it was like one of those dreams in which you take off from a balcony and discover that the air supports you. What, then, could remain of our constraints, our difficulties, her life, my life? Nothing. Only two fishes surrendered to the sea, surrendered to that water, drunk on it. Sometimes we came face to face with real fish. They looked at us, then moved away, some with a sudden twist of the body, others with a nonchalant flick of the fins. At one point, looking up from the bottom, I saw Creezy above me, lying stretched out, sprawling on the sea the way she sprawled on her bed when sleep had swallowed her up. The next moment she was several feet below me, lying on her back, gliding along, looking up at me. I saw her look, saw her wide eyes behind the mask, made to seem even wider by the mask, and a long way off, as if seen through a porthole. I swam down to her, swooped on her, our masks bumped, our legs intertwined, our bodies clung together, her hands on my waist, mine on her hips, her hard breasts pressed against my chest, the water sliding between our bodies like an extra caress, like another's caress, and the sea around us, supporting, protecting us in our wedding at the bottom of the sea, the sea our bed, the sea our house, the sea finally become our mother, and we her children, sheltering in her womb.

We swam back to the surface. The wind had sprung up. The sea, so smooth before, was like crumpled paper. Short, savage waves burst in our faces. I drove back at a furious speed. The boat smacked the water viciously. The waves were getting higher. The boat bucked, slipped sideways, and then the engines caught again with a roar, and, from behind me, bouncing around on the yellow cushions, Creezy shouted, "Bastard!" every time a wave splashed her.

Another day, after a long run, we stopped off an island. There was a little port there, with houses piled up on top of one another, ocher, gray, blue, bleached by the sun, no doors or windows, simply holes in the walls, as if eroded by the sea and the wind. Creezy dived. She brought up several specimens of an underwater creature neither of us had ever seen before. It looked just like a piece of rock, but in certain places it was soft to the touch. The flesh inside was orange and lemon-yellow; the flavor was fairly pleasant but it left a bitter after-taste. The sun set. The sky was green as we returned to our square tower. The caretaker's wife had laid the table on the terrace. She was an enormous woman with a piping voice, and instead of counting on her fingers she used to count on her nose, I mean with her fingers on her nose. Around us farm-yard sounds floated up through the olive trees: a cock, a few hens, a pig grunting in its sty. Also, during our stay, a heat wave settled on the district. The nights were like endless journeys, interrupted by sudden wakings, nightmares. I woke up. Creezy was no longer there. I found her on the terrace, her face searching for the cool breeze that seemed to have gone forever. Out over the sea, pale, silent flashes of lightning hung and flickered. In the end we made love, but with our nerves strained to the breaking point.

eighteen

Nothing altered my decision. During those eight days all our happiness returned. Not for one second did I lose sight of the fact that it was only temporary. We flew back to Nice and went on to Paris in my car. When we arrived at the apartment, Snow took Creezy's face in her hands and patted it tenderly. Then, as if to avoid any jealousy, she stroked my cheek.

The next morning she brought us breakfast in bed. I got dressed. I knew exactly what I had to do. I knew it must be done quickly. Creezy pushed the breakfast tray to one side and got up. She came toward me. In her wide, green eyes I saw the words, the night words, her monotonous demand: "Take me with you, take me with you." She said nothing; she cried out to me. She cried out to me from a great distance. And, from one second to the next, everything had tilted over. With a kind of terror, but terror in which there was also joy, in which there was also exultation, I felt myself uplifted by some emotion I didn't recognize. Those eight days, in which I believed I'd done nothing except be happy, now started to swamp me, to jostle me. We were back at the bottom of the sea. Free—as at the bottom of the sea. Everything that had seemed absurd to me no longer seemed absurd. Or criminal, no longer criminal. Forbidden, no longer forbidden. I could live with Creezy. I wanted to live with Creezy. I wanted to overwhelm Creezy with my love. For an instant I felt like a man tottering on the brink of a precipice. I felt acutely, in that instant, that I had a choice between saying only two things, both equally irrevocable.

I caught my breath again and finally said a third. I said, "I've got to go to Morlan."

"Today?"

"Yes, today. I must."

Dizzy, staggering, with that landslide going on inside me, I had to have something to hang on to, even if it was only my car, my steering wheel, the roar of the engine. Why had I said Morlan? What did I want with Morlan, then? But I felt I had to go there; it seemed to me that it would be appalling cowardice not to go there; it seemed to me that, faced with those eight days, I must see Betty once again, and that my decision must be made in front of her, even with her.

Once in my car I drove like a madman. I grabbed at anything. I studied license plates. Even—Creezy. Odd— Betty. I watched my speedometer. Even—Creezy. Odd— Betty. I told myself: think of your children. I told myself: think of Creezy, she needs you, it's her only reason for living.

I arrived in time for dinner. I looked around me, at the dining room, at Betty leaning over Coralie, at Antoine with his napkin tucked under his arms, a method Betty had discovered for teaching him not to eat with his elbows in the air. Did they still need me? I looked for a sign. There was no sign. There's never a sign.

I was tired, dead tired. I went to bed. For the first time in weeks I slept soundly. When I woke up my mind was clear. I went into Betty's room. She had laid out one of Coralie's dresses on the bed. She had a needle in her hand and she looked as if she was about to begin a particularly arduous game of chess. I said, "I must leave again." Then, very quickly, the way Creezy would have spoken, I added, "There's someone in Paris who needs me."

Betty looked at me for a moment, went over to her dressing table, stuck her needle into a spool of cotton and, without turning around, asked, "Will you be coming back?"

A second passed. It seemed to me I saw it pass, saw it come between us. I said, "No. No, I won't be coming back."

Then Betty said this: "How old is she?"

The question took me so much by surprise that I said, "Who?" It wasn't what I meant to say. I meant to say . . .

Betty turned around at last and said sharply, "I suppose it's that Creezy woman." It was as if this access of anger had liberated Betty. Her face no longer showed anything except a kind of curiosity. She looked at me as if she was seeing me for the first time. "You're a fool," she said.

I was a fool, I knew that. At that moment I was being wholly destructive. It was the work of a fool. I was destroying the bond with Betty, although just then I felt it with all its old force, and I felt too, with sorrow, that for her as well, without my having realized, it had begun to come apart. I was destroying the bond with my children. I knew they wouldn't understand. They wouldn't understand for a long time to come. I was destroying my life. I wasn't deputy for Paris. I was the deputy for Morlan. Divorced and remarried to Creezy, I knew I would never be re-elected. And what would happen to my legal practice didn't bear thinking about. What, then, was left for me? To be public relations officer for a fashion house? And I would have to renounce that passion of mine, that passion which no one, strangely, not one deputy, not one minister, will ever admit to—the passion for politics. I added, "Are you angry with me?"

I wished I could have taken it back. Suddenly, Betty's face came apart. She went out of the room. I could hear her going downstairs. I went through to my room. I picked up a few things and put them in my suitcase. There was an air of unreality about my actions. The things were not things; they were patches of mist, tufts of cloud. As I passed the telephone it occurred to me that I ought to give Creezy a call. But, as I said, the telephone was in the hall and everyone would have been able to hear. I couldn't do that to Betty.

Coralie was playing hopscotch in the garden. She wanted me to play as well. I played. I reached heaven. Which heaven? Antoine hailed me from the top of a pear tree, where he sat like a topman on his mast. I shouted back, "Be careful."

I drove away. I drove fast. I reached Paris. Parked outside Creezy's building was a twenty-foot-long, raspberry-colored car. The color was so glaring it made me smile at first. It wasn't even raspberry; it was crushed strawberry. Then, as I was pulling my key out of the ignition, something made me stop: at the wheel of the other car I had just recognized the frizzy-haired youth whom I'd seen rubbing down Sammy Minelli. And a moment later, running along the *opus incertum* path, I recognized Minelli himself.

I went up. In the hall I bumped into Snow, who greeted me a little too loudly. Savagely, I pushed her aside. I climbed the stairs. Creezy was sitting at her dressing table, wearing a white bathrobe. She raised her head. She looked at me in the mirror. Her face was caught in the mirror, caught in that sheet of ice, caught in that frozen pond, in that glacial universe which, despite all her efforts, was ours and always had been. That universe of the moment, without sequel, without warmth.

I went back down the stairs. I wanted to leave. Snow was still standing in the hall. She shook her head: No, no. She placed her hands together. I went out onto the balcony. I tried to discover what I felt. I felt nothing, neither anger nor sorrow, nothing but that sensation of collapse, that steel flower slowly opening inside my chest, nothing but the bitter conviction that I'd been right. Right to have been unwilling to venture farther into that desert. I stood there, leaning against the glass balustrade. Below me—the cliff, emptiness, twelve stories of it. It was the sly hour, the shifty hour, the hour of the wild beasts, the hour that was my enemy. The daylight was still battling with the light from the tall street lights.

Creezy was behind me. She came closer. She was touching me. And she said, "You weren't there." In an expressionless voice. A bleak voice. She said, "You weren't there."

All it needs, I thought, is one word, one gesture, from her, from me. There's too much, surely, between us, for one stupid mistake to destroy. One stupid mistake can't beat us. It did. Suddenly a poisonous darkness welled up inside me. I took Creezy in my arms. Already, against me, she was relaxed. I lifted her legs. Down below, very far off, a little boy was speeding past on his roller skates. I could hear the hiss of the skates. As quickly as it all happened, there was a moment when Creezy was simply waiting. Not a tremor crossed her face. My Creezy, my baby, my icon, my painted idol, my bird of paradise. I saw her last look. I dare to say that in that look there was nothing but an immense pity.

And I ran, I ran, I ran. Five stairs at a time, stumbling, falling over, knocking against the walls. At the bottom, outside the entrance, in the empty glare of the tall street lights, lay Creezy, her white bathrobe around her, one leg folded under her. I threw myself on her. Except for a trickle of blood, a very tiny one, at the corner of the mouth, her face was undamaged. Then a brutal light fell around us. Someone had switched on the entrance lights. And I could hear the concierge yelling. I turned and shouted, "Telephone! Get on and telephone!" Someone knelt beside me. It was Snow. She took Creezy's face in her hands. It was the same gesture she'd made two days before. She leaned forward, listened, and

slowly passed her hand over Creezy's eyelids. She said something I didn't understand. A car drew up. We were surrounded by policemen. Snow stood up and, without even
waiting for a question, immediately launched into a rapid,
vehement speech, full of shouts and exclamations and of which
I understood not a word. Which I didn't even try to understand. Any moment the policemen would pounce on me. I
didn't care. It was all happening a long way off. There lay my
Creezy, my life, that broken body, those closed eyes, that look
which I would never see again. One of the policemen bent over
me and lifted me to my feet. Another, evidently the chief, was
still listening to Snow. At one point he turned to me and said
very rapidly, as if in parentheses, "I usually spend my vaca-
tions on the Costa Brava." The words were so strange that it
took me a few minutes to understand what they meant: that
he understood Spanish, that he understood the gist of what
Snow was saying, and, to judge by his tone of voice, that
nothing of what she had said so far laid any blame on me. At
one point in her speech she even gave me a rapid glance, but it
conveyed nothing but respect. What had she told him? She
was still talking as rapidly as before, gesturing, beating her
breast, clutching her cheeks. She pointed at Creezy, she
pointed at me, but without looking in my direction. Her voice
became more and more vehement. It became a sob, a scream.
One of the policemen was now kneeling beside Creezy. He
looked up.

"All right," said the chief. "Where's the telephone?"

nineteen

Creezy's death was announced in the papers. Creezy's suicide. With banner headlines, enormous photographs, and articles that dripped home truths: fame is brittle, fame does not bring happiness. My name didn't appear once. I was at the Chamber. I thought the Minister of the Interior gave me rather a long look but I'm not even sure of that. I went home and found Betty there. She was giving instructions to a mover and he was packing up her things and the children's. She's left me the apartment. She'll live at Morlan, at least until the divorce comes through. We didn't mention Creezy. The woman before me wasn't Betty but a stranger, someone I didn't know. Someone I suddenly didn't know, who was suddenly a thousand miles away. It seemed to me as if there had never been anything between us, that we had perhaps never even met before, and that it was only by accident, or by some mistake, that her dresses and furs hung in my wardrobes.

I've had to pay another visit to police headquarters. Snow made no mention of Sammy Minelli in her statement. She didn't want him to have had any part in Creezy's life. From then on it was straightforward: "Monsieur came to the apartment. He told Mademoiselle he must leave her. Mademoiselle went out on the balcony and shouted, 'If you leave me I'll throw myself off.' Monsieur was standing by the front door. He said, 'No, you won't.' He turned to me and said, 'I leave her in your hands, Snow; look after her.' Then he left. I ran to Mademoiselle. I was too late."

The superintendent walked with me to my car. He said, "Happens all the time, this sort of thing. Nothing you can do about it. We ought to have more sense. Can't call it living though, can you, being sensible?"

I've been to see Snow. She didn't appear to understand a word of what I was trying to tell her. She said, "Mademoiselle so kind." Then she sat down and began to cry, softly, the thin tears running down her bony face. Then she said a lot more things which I still didn't understand. By the end I gathered that she'd had enough, her grief was too great, she wanted to go home, back to Spain, and she had no money. At that point a base idea occurred to me. I said, "Snow, wait. I come back." Making signs. I went to my bank. I took out a large sum of money. Snow looked astonished when she saw it. She said, "No, not right," but without indignation, like someone faced with a simple error of arithmetic. She took six hundred francs, the amount of her wages, and then, shyly, as if she wasn't too sure of herself, as if she was afraid of imposing, but with a kind of . . . a kind of mischievousness, she took another three hundred francs and made a circular movement with both arms, like a child playing trains, to intimate that that was the price of her ticket. There we sat, in the living area, the money lying between us on the lowered table, surrounded by that emptiness, that huge, cold, empty cube, the great window wall, the posters, the television set. Was it really me sitting there? My Creezy, my baby, my bird of paradise, was it me who killed you? And whom did I kill? Neon, plastic,